DEADLY

LITTLE

PAWN

The Daring Sisterhood

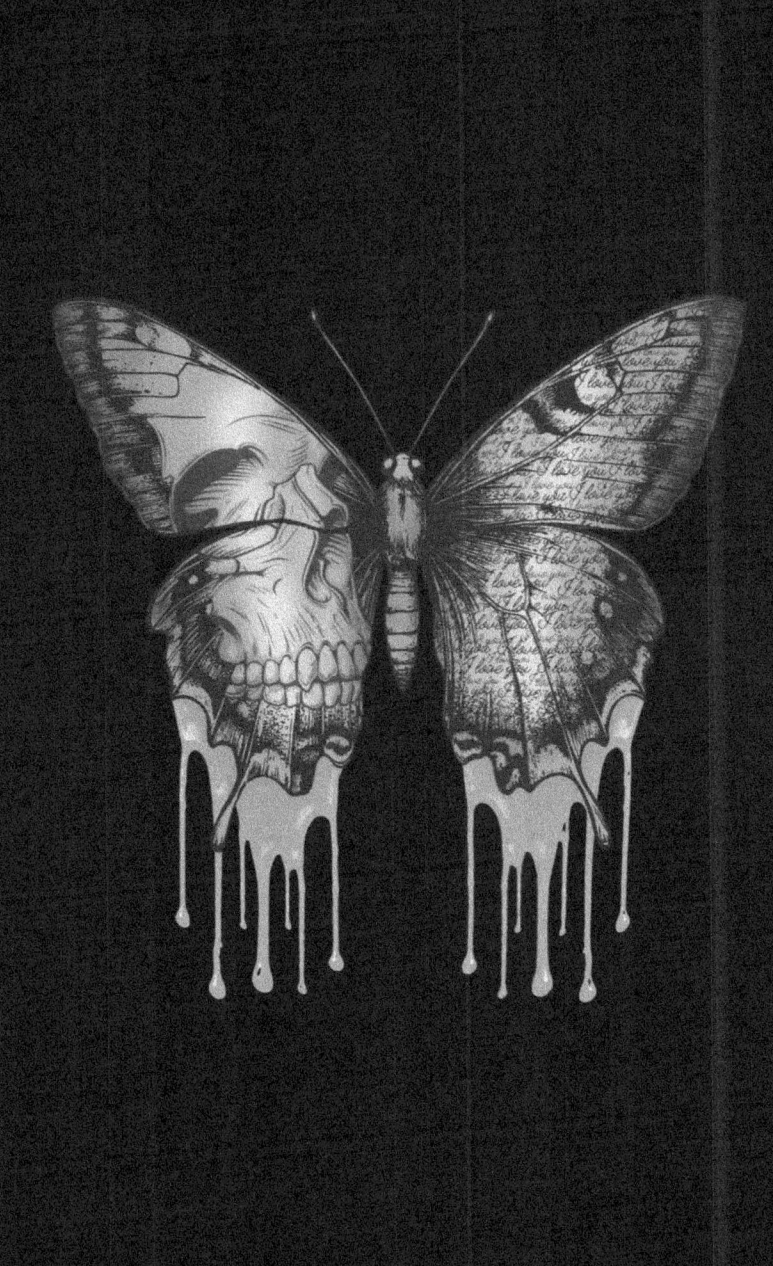

Published by The Daring Press

Cover Designer: Dark Romance Realm

Editors: Creating Ink, Autumn Reed Book Editing and Messengers Memos

CONTENTS

DEADLY LITTLE PAWN

In Daringhood, pawns aren't meant to survive the game. Especially when you're the princess of The Daring Brotherhood.

Amirah never wanted to be part of her brother's war. She has her own mission—saving women who've been taken from their families, refusing to let another girl vanish. But the moment she's stolen from her home and locked inside an abandoned theme park, her fight isn't for others anymore. It's for herself.

Her captor? Bear. Brutal. Unhinged. Obsessed. He swears she belongs to him but in the darkness, obsession can look a lot like devotion.

Her jailer's ally? Kai. This vengeful, haunted man sees her as a bargaining chip for redemption, even as every glance from her threatens to unravel his resolve. He's torn between protecting his own and protecting her.

Then there's Zion. He's loyal to no one but his blood. Amirah is a liability—and now she knows his deepest secret. Yet when she puts herself at risk to save someone he loves, lines blur, and the pawn becomes a playing piece he just can't ignore.

War between the Brotherhood and Daringhood is erupting, and Amirah is caught at its center.

She refuses to break. She refuses to kneel. But in a world where pawns are sacrificed first, every choice could be her last.

And in the end, even princesses bleed.

This is the first book in The Daring Sisterhood duet and part of The Daring Brotherhood interconnected series. Recommended to read Deadly Little Games and Deadly Little Hearts first but not a deal breaker.

TRIGGER WARNINGS

Deadly Little Pawn contains themes that may be distressing for some readers, including:

Kidnapping and captivity

Psychological manipulation and mind games

Violence and gang warfare

Threats of sexual violence (off-page)

Power imbalance and coercive dynamics

Trauma responses, panic, and fear

Emotional abuse and control

Dark romantic themes and morally grey characters

This is a dark romance.

Nothing is gentle.

Nothing is accidental.

Please read with care and only if you're ready to walk into the depths of hell.

You've been warned...

For the ones who survive by writing it out.

Who sit alone with their demons and give them names.

Who turn chaos into words, pain into power and madness into meaning.

This story is for you.

CHAPTER ONE

Bear

I lost my little puppy dog tonight, and I'm hunting him down. Lucas Fox, the bright and shiny golden retriever of The Daring Brotherhood, isn't getting away from me. No one ever does. He's my favorite captive yet, and our time isn't done. He can't run away from me. I'll drag him back by his tail and tie him to my ass.

I grin. That I'd love to see.

I blend into the darkness of the night behind the trees on the street corner, five blocks from the tracks. About twenty feet away from me, Lucas yells at a girl with long dark hair, telling her to go home. Her fists tighten at her sides as her eyebrows draw together, making her look like she wants to fight back, but she doesn't. Interesting little creature. She's dressed in all black, with tight pants that hug every curve.

I'm hypnotized by her, watching her from a distance. She's strong, her body language screaming *tough bitch*. Her long, straight dark hair hangs loose down her back. The urge to wrap it around my wrist and pull until each strand falls from her skull is strong.

I've seen her before. She's the princess of The Daring Brotherhood—Gage Ledger's sister, Amirah. Her name rolls off my tongue effortlessly, sounding like a nursery rhyme. Gage is one of the new leaders of The Brotherhood, so by all accounts, she's a high-value commodity. Taking her would hurt The Brotherhood more than taking Lucas. I'm captivated by her; she would be way more fun to play with. And Kai would be proud too. He wanted Freya—I'll give him another pussy instead.

Though she's been around with Freya, I haven't really seen her until now. She looks fun.

I know women like her. She'll be out partying late at night, every night, drinking her tequila from gold-lined shot glasses, covered in body glitter and all that shit before she bathes in Armani perfume and sleeps with some overly waxed male model who probably rides bicycles for fun.

Or that's who she should be—a princess.

But there's something different about her, a strength in her eyes I wasn't expecting.

The pawn could be deadly. Fuck Lucas. Amirah, it is.

Shaking my head, I flick off the ash from my smoke and lean back on my motorcycle. Dried blood from my fight with Lucas stains my white shirt even here in the shadows, where there's little moonlight.

After bringing the fabric over my head, I shove the end of the T-shirt into my pants pocket. Lucas stabbed me earlier before running back to Daringville like a widdle puppy. I liked him. He was fun to play with, but now he's gone and I'm sad. But I have a new mission, one that lights my insides on fire.

Fuck, it feels good. The burning sensation inside my stomach, the way the blade sliced through my skin. Fuck. I live for pain. If I don't have it, then it doesn't feel like I'm alive. I sewed the wound up with my needle and thread. It's going to leave a gnarly scar—a reminder of my precious time with my little pup, Lucas Fox.

Kill her, the voice inside me whispers, and I crack my neck, squeezing my eyes shut.

Maybe I will. I want to hunt her down first. Bend her, teach her, see how far I can push her. She's different. Taking her will hurt them, and that's all that matters.

The voice quiets down again, so I can focus back on her. The rumble of her car rips through the night, and Lucas walks away toward the house. She's leaving. *No.* Dropping the rest of my smoke to the ground, I wrap my leg over my bike and kick the lever. She roars to life, and I follow Amirah's car, keeping my lights off. I don't want her to see me. Not yet. I want to surprise her, to take her when she least expects it.

Excitement builds inside me. My fingers wrap around the bars. I keep a good distance between her and me as we cruise the quiet streets of Daringville, the cookie-cutter mansions flying past. Stupid rich people having shit they don't need.

She reaches the entrance to a rich estate, and I leave my bike half a block away before running closer. My stitches burn with each step, a reminder that I'm alive.

As the gate opens and she drives through, I creep round the guard block before sneaking through the open gates. He doesn't even notice me—so much for over-the-top security. Fools.

Sticking close to the tree line next to the road, I follow her down a long driveway. The garage door opens, revealing a gallery-like display of cars and bikes. She parks in the garage and drool runs down my chin. So many cars, bikes. Fuck. I want 'em all. Maybe I can take one of them home? Or all of them?

No, we just want her. Focus. The voices are right; she's my priority.

There are a couple members of The Brotherhood moving around the perimeter of the house a short distance from where I am in the tree line, but they haven't spotted me yet. The garage door starts to close. I watch the guards closely, and when one turns to talk to the other, I make my move. I sprint a hundred feet from the tree line and roll under the garage door with only inches to spare. They should have planned their yard better. All this space, and they put hedges this close to the house? Anyone could—and I will—break in. Idiots. My skin itches and my eyes roll into the back of my head.

It takes everything in me not to grab the keys to the Ecosse ES1 Spirit superbike and leave. Fuck me. There are more cars and bikes than I can count, all worth millions. I run my hands over the metal of the motorcycle, a jolt of electricity pulsing through me.

We want her.

Right. I need to focus.

I stalk toward the white door at the end of the garage and twist the knob ever so slightly before opening it a crack. As I peer inside the house, it's quiet. Light streams down from the stairs, and I make my move, stalking up them two at a time to follow the golden glow. I reach a door that's half open.

There she is, talking with another woman who's wearing a black-and-white-checkered dress—a maid, most likely. Fucking rich people. We're over in the Hood, struggling to afford our next meal, and here they are living with more than they could ever need. The system is fucked.

Amirah grabs the lady's arm, handing her a wad of cash. Her eyes widen before she shakes her head, but Amirah shoves the money inside her front pocket. They talk in hushed tones that I can't hear through the door. Amirah hugs her and she returns it.

She's helping the maid? Why?

I need to know her.

We all do.

The maid wipes away her tears and hugs Amirah again before coming toward me. Fuck. I push back against the wall next to the door. She moves out of what must be Amirah's bedroom and heads in the opposite direction without seeing me. My heartbeat skyrockets. She could notice me at any second. She puts some earbuds in before descending the stairs, and it's not long before the slam of the front door echoes back toward me. She's gone. Perfect, I can focus on Amirah.

I let out a heavy sigh, then peer back in at Amirah. She is sprawled out on her bed, her dark hair fanned out over her pillow. She's furiously typing away on her phone, her brows scrunched together.

My dick hardens watching her. Her tight black top rides up as she shifts positions, showing off her toned stomach.

Get her. Claim her now.

The voices inside my head are trying to stake their claim. *Shut up.*

Those wide hips . . . I want to bite her ass, leaving my teeth marks there as a reminder of who she belongs to. She doesn't even know me yet, but she will.

She will be ours.

She's my new obsession. My heart hammers against my rib cage. The excitement—I haven't felt it this strong before. She's going to be fun.

No, we want her dead.

Shut up, she's my toy first.

Using my boot, I kick open the door.

Amirah's eyes clash with mine, widening before she screams, "Who the hell are you?!"

My pulse kicking up a notch, I pull the door shut behind me and rush toward her. She rolls off the mattress, standing between me and her bed. She screams again.

"Shut up," I say, moving closer until I reach the end of her bed.

She steps backward, watching me closely. I look to the other side of the bed, to her phone sitting there. I stalk over and grab it before she can, shoving it into my pants pocket.

She curses and runs toward the door.

"I wouldn't if I were you. One move, and I'll run this blade across your sweet cheeks."

Amirah stops at the door. She turns around and walks slowly back to the bed opposite me. Good girl.

The corner of my mouth lifts as I undress her with my gaze, moving from her tight black pants up her curves.

Touch her.

I can't, not yet.

Her chest rises and falls at a rapid rate. What feels like a thousand moths flutter inside my stomach. What the fuck is that about?

Being this close to her, watching her body react to me. Does she feel whatever this is between us too? It's confusing. She's different, and I want to know everything about her.

Her eyes flick from me to the door, and before she can move, I'm on her. Jumping over the bed, I pull her down onto the mattress, then pin her by grabbing her arms and sitting on her hips. She thrashes around, rubbing her cunt all over my cock. Fuck me sideways.

"If you wanna fuck, I'm down," I offer, and her wild eyes glare right into my soul.

"Get the fuck off me now!" Her voice rises with each word.

She's strong; she will be my greatest captive.

No, kill her and leave, the voice begs.

I shake my head furiously, and Amirah watches me closely with her mossy-green eyes. There's not fear but curiosity beaming from her gaze. I need to know her, to play with her. To go into the depths of who she really is behind her exterior. Usually when I take someone, they cry. They kick and scream, but fear—it's always lurking in their eyes.

She's not afraid.

She's pissed off, and it's fucking sexy. I can't let her go now. I need to know who she is.

Leaning down, I bring my nose to her neck. Her body stills. Her heart races against mine. She wants this—the way her body reacts to mine is electrifying. Magnetic. As though our souls are connected.

"I recognize you. Aren't you Kai's friend, Bear?"

She recognizes me? No one ever sees me. All the ville people see is Kai—I'm just the muscle. The other one. The crazy one. Why would someone like her see me?

"No," I reply quickly. The irony of the one time someone *does* see me being the one time I wish they didn't is not lost on me.

Her soft skin smells of grapefruit. I run my nose along her neck, and my eyes roll into the back of my head. Fuck. She's electrifying. The way her body reacts to mine, every curve molding into every part of me. Does she know how close she is to death? Doesn't she know I'm a monster—and women like her don't fuck men like me?

"Get off me," she says, her voice breaking.

"You want me, princess. One taste and you'll be hooked." My words ring through the quiet room.

She shuffles on the bed, moving her hips. I give her a little room, and pain erupts in my balls. I fall sideways, my hands cupping my groin. She kicks me in the stomach, right over my wound. Pain radiates through my body. I taste it—the sick feeling that too much hurt can bring.

But she doesn't know that I like it.

Before I can right myself, she rolls off the bed and runs, heading straight for her bathroom.

A full grin plays on my lips. Cheeky princess wants to play with me. *Punish her.*

I will.

The bathroom door slams shut, followed by a click of the lock. My eyes roll—like a lock is going to stop me. The big bad wolf is going to knock it down, but I don't want to damage her in the process.

When I cause her pain, I want to see it in her eyes.

Pressing my ear against the door, I hear her heavy breathing on the other side. I place my hand next to my head.

"Oh, princess, won't you let me in? I just want to play with you. You're making this big bad wolf very sad," I whine, pushing out my bottom lip.

"You're crazy. My brother will be in to check on me any moment now. Don't you know who I am?" She bangs her fist against the door, the vibration rolling over my skin. "Leave now while you still can."

I smile at her words. She cares about me. Aww.

"Stand back, princess. I'm going to blow this castle down."

I retreat a step and wait a few seconds before my foot connects with the wood. Once, then twice. The door shakes but doesn't budge. With one last kick, the door swings open, smashing against the wall with a heavy crack. Shit. Guards will hear that. I'm gonna have to hustle.

I step inside, my chest pumping heavily. There she is, standing in front of the mirror with a razor blade in her grip, blood dripping over her porcelain skin.

She stares at me, her eyes wild with hate and anger. My cock stirs. My lips tilt up as I step farther inside. She doesn't cower; she holds her place. None of my captives have ever fought back like this. *I think we're in love.*

"Let me leave and I won't hurt you," she says, and I laugh, my boot touching her bare foot. She doesn't quiver, her fingers curling around the razor just an inch from my chest. A drop of blood runs down her fingers, and I want a taste. I bet she's sweet.

"Aww, I won't hurt you, princess." I sigh, reaching out and tucking a piece of her wild black hair behind her ear. Her skin burns and she doesn't pull away. "I'm going to take you with me. You're going to be my new favorite toy. My prized possession."

She swats away my hand, bringing the razor blade up to my throat. Her green eyes turn dark. The moths return to my stomach, fluttering their wings.

"I'm no one's possession," she growls.

Blood trickles down my neck the harder she pushes. I want to bleed for her, watch her run her tongue along my skin and taste every last drop. *Would she?*

We don't need permission. We'd make her, and she'd love it.

The hair on my skin raises at the thought of her touching me like that.

We need to go now. We're done waiting.

"Shut up!" I yell, squeezing my eyes shut before taking a heavy exhale, then opening them. She looks at me, frowning.

Before I take my next breath, I grab her wrist, twisting until she drops the blade. It falls onto the vanity next to her. Her sweet blood drips over her delicate skin—clean skin—painting her red. I lick my dry lips.

Just one taste. Then we can go.

She thrashes against me, trying to break free. In one movement, I grab her waist, lift her up, and place her on the counter. After snatching her wrist, I bring it to my lips, running my tongue over her palm, collecting every single drop. My eyes roll into the back of my head. Sweet, tangy, and so divine.

She sucks in a breath. "Get the fuck off me!" she yells, then screams.

The high pitch bleeds into my skull. *She needs to shut up. Now.* Dropping her hand, I shake my head furiously, trying to stop the voice inside my head. *Hurt her. Punish her. Or are you too weak?*

It's all too much. I need to get out of here. I need to release the hold the voices have on me.

"My brother and our guards will be back soon, and if he finds you here, you're dead. Just go, and I won't say a word. Promise." She stares at me, her green eyes turning a softer shade, and for a moment, I believe her. But that's silly of me. Words are mere distractions; she doesn't mean what she said. The second he's back, she'll talk.

She's mine now, and I won't be leaving without her.

CHAPTER Two

A mirah

My chest rises and falls to the rate of my pounding heart. I'm staring into his bright-green eyes, watching and waiting to see what he does next.

How the fuck did he get in here? If only every man and his dog wasn't out helping my brother right now, this wouldn't have happened.

But I don't need a man to save me.

They weren't there for me when I needed them, and I sure as shit won't wait for them to rescue me now.

I have to get away from him. I need to leave. He's unpredictable, and if I make one wrong move, I have no doubt, from that gleam in his eyes, that he'll kill me.

If I can get away from him, run down the stairs and scream for help, surely one of the guards will hear me. Or I'll just run until I'm far away from him. Out of his reach. I'm not strong enough to fight him off. He's bigger than me. Stronger.

My gaze moves from Bear to the bathroom door. If I can just make it there, I'm halfway out. If I can get out of my room and down the stairs, I can alert someone. Maria has gone home—I let her go early to be with her family. But there are still some guards here; Gage didn't leave me alone.

I have to play this smart. Distract him long enough to make my move. When he tasted my blood, his eyes shut, and he went to another place. Bile rises in my throat at the thought.

As part of one of the founding families of The Brotherhood, I've been surrounded by men my entire life. Men who have been kind, vile, twisted, but I have *never* met someone like Bear. I can't read him. He's staring off into space, like he's somewhere else. I don't know whether he wants to kill me or hug me.

I need to get away from him before it's too late. I need to distract him. And men like him—they're all driven by sex. They think that's all we're good for.

I'm going to use his weakness against him.

I reach out, bringing my bleeding palm closer to Bear's mouth. He watches me, cocking his head to the side.

"I want you to lick off all my blood. Make it clean for me, please?" I ask in my sweetest tone.

The corner of his mouth curves up, his green eyes brightening. I've got him, hook, line, and sinker.

His tongue slides over my skin. Goosebumps scatter along my arms, and I forget for several seconds what I'm supposed to do, distracted by the way his tongue lights me on fire. His eyes never leave mine, like they are holding me in place. Fuck. There's something almost . . . almost erotic about this moment.

I've never been touched by a man like this before.

Fuck. No. I'm supposed to be escaping. Shaking my head, I take one deep breath. Now or never. He's focused on cleaning up my bloody palm, so I reach for the razor with my other hand. If I can just move one more inch—it's so close. I feel the edge of the blade, and it pricks my finger.

Move. Now.

I fall sideways, grabbing the razor and wrapping my palm around it. Pain bites into my skin, but I ignore it. Twisting back around, I stab the razor blade into his chest, and it bites into his already wounded torso. He moans. I kick up my foot, connecting with Bear's balls. He stumbles back slightly, and it's all I need.

I roll off the counter and run toward the bathroom door. Pain erupts in my scalp as I'm pulled backward, hitting a wall of muscle. The razor blade drops from my hand, and Bear kicks it out of reach. *No!*

His breath tickles my neck. I squirm, trying to break free, but I can't. His grip on my hair tightens and my vision blurs. If I can just make it out this door, I'll be free.

Ignoring the pain, I slam down my foot, connecting with his boot, and launch forward. I get one step before his hand wraps around the back of my neck and he shoves me forward. My forehead smashes into the wall.

Pain bleeds through my scalp, and my vision blurs at the edges.

Just before I lose consciousness, a voice reaches me. His voice.

"Bad little princess. Say good night. Your fairy tale starts now."

CHAPTER THREE

Before - Ten Years Old

Amirah

She's gone. She left me, us. Why didn't she want me anymore? What did I do wrong?

I thought Mom loved me, but she didn't. Not really. She always looked at me with sad eyes. She didn't want to be here with us. Ever since Daddy died, she's been different. He always made her cry, but she never left him or us—until now. If Mom is gone and Dad's dead, am I an orphan? It doesn't feel any different than before. She's never been around for long; it's always been Gage and me.

She went away for short trips, but this time when I saw her bags packed at the front door, it felt different. When she told my nanny, Lily, to keep me safe, my heart hurt. No one can truly keep me safe here.

My big brother Gage always protects me from the bad guys, but he can't be everywhere. They still come in the night. Hurting me. Telling me to be quiet and not to scream. I want to. It always hurts. Nightmares aren't real, but *they* are.

As the door to my bedroom opens, I sit up straight, my shoulders tensing, and I rush to wipe away my tears. I relax back into my pillows when I see Lily, my nanny. She never judges me; she loves me. Everything is better when she's here.

A mop of red hair peers out from behind her, and I smile.

"Jewel," I say, and she pushes past her mother and jumps onto my bed, falling next to me. I giggle, and it feels good.

Lily shuts the door and comes over and sits on the edge of the bed. "You okay, sweetie?" she asks, and memories of this morning flood my mind once more. Of my mother walking out the door. More tears leak from my eyes. She left me.

Lily pulls me into her arms. I rest my head on her heart, listening to the soft thumping. Jewel kneels in front of us, resting her hand on my knee.

"Is she ever coming back?" My voice wobbles, my chest burning.

"Not this time," Lily whispers, and more tears soak into her shirt. She continues to hold me for what feels like forever. When my tears dry, I pull back, and Lily places her hands on my shoulders, looking at me with a sad smile.

"You will always have me," she says, and I believe her; she's always there for me.

The bed shifts. "And me." Jewel wraps her arm over my shoulder, pushing me sideways. I fall onto my arm, a tiny laugh escaping me as she tickles me.

"You two play. I've got some cleaning to do. Okay?" Lily tucks a piece of my dark hair behind my ear, and her palm rests on my cheek.

I don't want her to leave, too, but I know she'll be back. Still, it's hard not to clutch her hand tight, to keep her here with me. Instead, I nod, and she leaves.

Jewel bounces off the bed, pulling me with her toward the corner of my room where all my dolls are. We love playing with dolls, creating stories about princesses and nice princes.

It helps me forget about the bad guys in my real life, because princesses and princes don't exist here.

CHAPTER FOUR

A^{mirah}

A loud squeal pierces my ears, getting louder and louder. I groan, reaching for my alarm clock, but my hand lands on cool metal. Wind brushes my hair away from my face, getting stronger and stronger.

It takes me a second to peel my eyes open, and when I do, I'm looking down to my death. Clasping onto the railing, I scream. My breath comes in and out in short bursts. I try to move, but the strap around my waist keeps me in place. I'm high above the ground, sitting on a rusty roller-coaster cart. It moves up and up, the metal clicking and squealing.

Darkness surrounds me, and it's hard to see. Little lights scatter along the railing of the roller coaster, but they don't do much.

Where the fuck am I? The last thing I remember is being with Kai's friend, Bear . . . I'm sure that's his name. It suits him. He's big, and danger radiates from him. I was trying to escape, then everything went black, and now here I am—strapped into an old fucking roller coaster, about to fall into the unknown. No, this can't be happening.

The cart comes to a stop. Wind surges around me. This is it, the calm before the storm. I'm going to die. Everything I've been through in my life comes down to this very moment.

I think of all the fun I've had. Sneaking my best friend Freya into parties and swimming at the beach together. Of going to school and acing every class. Of Jewel—of what I did.

Of all the things I haven't yet experienced and now will never have a chance to.

I won't be able to do all the important things I still want to accomplish.

"Smile." Bear's voice echoes from a speaker in front of me, through the otherwise quiet air.

I frown, shaking my head furiously before a bright light blinds me from somewhere in front of me. I shield my eyes, then it's gone, darkness consuming me once more.

"This is your captain speaking. Hold on tight. You're in for a fright." A robotic voice comes through a speaker somewhere in my cart.

My hands clench the safety bar in front of me. The old rust bites into my cut skin. Am I about to drop to my death? Will the safety belt around my waist fail me? What's waiting at the bottom? I don't know, and that frightens me.

There's still so much I want to do in this world. I try to release the strap around me, but my fingers shake and I can't get it loose.

Before I take my next breath, I'm falling. I hang on to the bar in front of me with all my might as my hair flings back over my shoulders. My screams and the squealing of metal against metal pierce my ears.

Bright-white light blinds me once again, then I'm sucked into a dark tunnel. The wind disappears, and I'm left with my heavy breathing. The cart jerks to a stop, and I fly forward. My breath leaves my body as the seat belt bites into my skin. Darkness surrounds me everywhere I look.

"Amirah Ledger, you're about to enter a restricted zone. Only those invited may enter. Please ensure you leave all belongings behind—you won't be needing them anymore. It's time to say goodbye to your old life and say hello to your new home: Dareland." The robotic voice sends waves of unease through my body.

My sweaty palms slip on the railing. Dareland—now that doesn't sound like fun. If Bear is running his own amusement park, there's no way I'll make it out of here alive. I remember when I saw him at the tracks that he cut his own lip open just for fun. He's a psycho.

My hands claw at my seat belt, trying to find the buckle. I can't see anything. Cool metal meets my fingers, and I attempt to lift the lever. I wiggle my hips, but the belt doesn't budge. Fuck. I frantically try again and again, but it doesn't release.

We're moving again. I slump back into my seat. A mixture of tears and sweat runs down my cheeks. We stop, and the speaker somewhere in my cart crackles.

"Knock, knock," the voice says, and I refuse to answer.

I'm not playing his games. I bring my bottom lip between my teeth.

"Who's there? That's what you're supposed to ask, princess."

I freeze. Maybe if I'm still enough, some other delusion will enter his mind, and he'll leave me alone.

Even as I think it, I know there's no chance.

"The Dare Land!"

Curtains are pulled away, bright lights and vibrant colors blinding me. It takes a second for the blurriness to disappear, and when it does, I want it to come back. This is too much.

A massive open clown's mouth with missing teeth stares back at me. Fake blood drips from its bottom lip. The track continues through his gaping mouth, and I want to turn around. Where's the fucking exit sign?

The cart pushes forward, and once again, I'm falling. We drop headfirst through the mouth, and then I'm surrounded by my own reflection. I'm in a room full of mirrors inside the world's creepiest clown. There I am, sitting in the old cart, sweat dripping down my face. My dark hair sticking to my skin. My eyes widened in horror.

I want to get off this ride right fucking now. I'm done. My poor heart can't handle anymore.

Yes, you can. You've been through worse.

The voices are right. I have, and I *will* get through this. No matter how challenging it's going to be or how far Bear is going to push me, I will get through this. I have to. People are relying on me, and I won't let them down. *I can't.*

The mirrors disappear and are replaced with checkerboards everywhere I look. My stomach lurches. I'm going to puke. Dizziness consumes me, and I lean over the edge. I need fresh air. The tunnel—or whatever the hell I'm in—is hot and stuffy, as though all the air has been sucked out.

"My precious princess, you are doing so well. Hang in there. All will be over soon."

I block out the voice, giving him nothing in return. The cart keeps moving me along the tracks, and the room switches again. Clowns in all shapes and sizes watch me, some with half their faces gone.

Their eyes stare right through me. I fucking hate clowns. They are evil. Crazy. Much like Bear.

I'm going up again, and I know what that means. What goes up must come down. The cool night air kisses my cheeks. As I reach the top of the roller coaster, I close my eyes. I don't want to see what's next. I slow down my breathing as best I can.

A loud thud fills my ears, then the cart rocks. What the hell was that? I grip the bar harder. I turn to my right, and a large shadow hovers next to me. Shit. My hands shake.

"Open those eyes. I need to see you." Bear's voice sounds so close, like he's right next to me.

A hand covers my mouth, muffling my screams. What the fuck? Where did he come from? Did he just drop in? Is that what that thud was?

The bar is pushed forward, my seat belt is lifted off, and I'm shoved onto his lap. His arms wrap around my body, holding me in place. I'm paralyzed, my hands shaking uncontrollably.

His hot breath hits my neck, his tongue sliding over my jawline. Goosebumps scatter over my skin, even though I'm burning hot. *Stop it. He's my enemy*, I try to convince my body, but she doesn't understand. She's responding to him like a horny teenager.

"You taste so sweet, princess. I can't wait to eat you."

I bite into Bear's finger, but he doesn't remove his hand from my mouth. He chuckles while wrapping his fingers tighter around me. The tangy taste of blood hits my tongue. At least I made him bleed.

"Let's see how wet you are," Bear whispers into my ear.

He isn't asking for permission, and I won't give it to him. I shake my head, squirming against him, trying to break free. But even if I did, where the fuck would I go? There's nowhere to escape to. I'm stuck here on this cart, suspended high above the ground, waiting for the roller coaster's descent.

His fingers reach my waistband, and my whole body locks up. I can't move. I can't breathe. He pushes inside, running his finger down my wet slit. My eyes shut. My pussy is begging him to touch her. What the fuck? No, I didn't ask for this. I didn't want this, but my body reacts to him in a way that's never happened before. I'm soaked, and I hate myself for it.

"My oh my, princess, how wet you are."

His words send shivers through my entire body. We start to descend, picking up speed. Without a second thought, I place my hand over his and guide his finger inside me. I need a diversion, and this way, he's not taking control of me. I'm taking control of him.

My skin feels alive at his touch. My heart beats to the clicking of the cart. I ride his fingers, pleasure swirling in tighter spirals in my belly. I scream. My hair flies around my face, blocking out everything around us.

"You're going to be my favorite captive yet."

I ignore him and squeeze my eyes shut, rubbing my thumb over my clit while guiding the movement of his fingers inside me. I'm almost there, and even though it's probably sick and twisted, I need this. Need some kind of high to distract my mind from the fear. Need my body to control him.

We come to a sudden stop, the cart squealing. Bear tries to yank his hand out, but I keep him in place. "Don't you dare. You owe me," I growl.

Bear chuckles and roughly pulls his hand away, taking mine with him. He grabs my hips, flipping me around so I'm facing him. His bright-green eyes stare straight through me. He's hot, there's no doubt about that, and the way my body reacts to him should be illegal.

He's my enemy, and I hate him for taking me away from my home, my family, but if he wants me to play his stupid games, then I'll make sure I win.

He may think I'm just a naïve Brotherhood princess, but he'll soon discover that I'm much more deadly than that.

I'll be his worst nightmare.

CHAPTER FIVE

B ear

The more time I spend in her presence, the more fixated I become. I thought she'd break going through my carnival, but she didn't. She's still here, in one piece. She's strong. I meant it when I said she's going to be my favorite captive yet. I can't wait to challenge her, to make her play my games and see how far I can really push her. To go deep inside her psyche, pick her apart until there's nothing left of her. Until I reach the very core of who she is. Her soul is going to be mine. I'll suck it out of her vessel and put it in a jar to keep.

Excitement builds inside me to the point where I need a release, but first, she needs hers. It's her reward for being such a good girl for her captor. With pain comes pleasure.

After grabbing her pussy from the outside of her pants, I forcefully rub my thumb over her clit. She glares, the little crease in her forehead deepening. She's telling me to hurry the fuck up. The way her body reacts to my touch is everything. It feels like pure ecstasy, taking me to the highest cliff.

She grabs my shoulder, her fingers digging into my skin. "Stop playing around," she huffs, and the corner of my mouth lifts.

"Tell me what you want, princess."

"To go home."

I squeeze her crotch harder, and her eyes flutter closed. "And you're a fucking liar."

Her hand connects with my face. Pain kisses my cheek, and my cock stirs.

"You know I've chopped off limbs for less," I say, and her eyes fly open.

Her chest rises and falls rapidly. "And if you don't get me off, I'll bite off your dick." She raises her perfectly manicured eyebrow, and fuck me, I want her to.

"You say it like it's a threat. Baby, that's a dream." I grin.

"Shut up and get me off. Give me something. I'm bored." She fake yawns, and I forcefully shove my hand back down her pants. Right into her warm cunt. Running my fingers through her wetness.

Her hands grip my shoulders, digging in. Her face showcases a mixture of fear and satisfaction. She's a puzzle to me, and I'm so fucking glad she appeared when she did. I needed a distraction. Someone to make me forget what I did. Someone to challenge me.

I push two fingers inside her, and her back arches, her mouth opening slightly before she slams it shut. She doesn't want me to see how much I affect her, and I revel in the power I have over her body now.

Her pussy clenches around my fingers, her juices pooling down my hand, and I can't wait to taste her. My cock begs for me to touch it, but this isn't about me—it's about her. Giving her exactly what she desires. I love a woman who knows what she wants. She's my captive. Mine. Ours.

I pick up my pace. She moans. Her fingers tangle in my hair, pulling my head back. Her gaze meets mine, and I get lost in her mossy-green eyes. I can't look away. She's mesmerizing. No one has ever made us feel like this. It's weird. Forbidden. Right. Confusing. I don't like it. She's making me feel things I don't understand. But I can't stop. I need to give her what she desires.

I push my thumb against her clit, rubbing while my fingers fuck her cunt. She's close. Her pupils dilate, and her grip in my hair gets more forceful.

Her mouth opens and the tiniest moan escapes, a sound I bottle up in my memories to replay later when I've got my hand wrapped around my cock.

I keep going until her release paints my hand. I pull out of her underwear and bring my fingers to my lips, then I lick off every last drop of her sweet tang.

My eyes roll into the back of my head. Holy mother of all things dark, she's the best meal I've ever had.

Her warmth disappears from my lap, and I reach out for her, grabbing her arm. She's halfway out of the cart, glaring at me with so much hatred. I lick my wet lips, not wanting to miss any of her release.

"Well, princess, do you feel good now?" I ask with a wink.

She rolls her eyes, pulling out of my grip. "I've had better."

All the happiness gets sucked from my veins. Her words feel like a knife to my cock. My heart squeezes, and I have no idea why. No one has ever had this effect on me before.

Looking after this princess is going to be one hell of an adventure.

CHAPTER SIX

Before - two weeks ago

Amirah

The four walls feel like they are closing in around me. My bedroom used to be my sanctuary, a place I'd go to escape and retreat. Now it feels like a prison. Gage, Lucas, and Hazen have taken the throne, and I'm torn with how I feel about it.

It's always been my brother's destiny to take over and become one of the leaders of The Brotherhood, but I didn't want to lose him completely to it. Over the years, the more he trained, the further apart we drifted. He doesn't like to admit that, and I don't either, but we both know The Brotherhood always comes first. They are our found family.

Gage has always been my protector; he's done everything he can to keep me safe. Every time I had a nightmare or needed him, he'd be there. But now it's different. I'm no longer a little kid. He's not here, and I don't need him anymore.

I squeeze my eyes shut, leaning deeper into the pillow. I'm going crazy in here. The silence is deafening. I want to reach out to Freya and ask her to come over, but with her mother trying to get clean, grieving her brother's death, and trying to mend Lucas's broken heart, she's got enough to deal with.

Every time I call her and ask if I can help her in any way, she says no. I still check in every day, just to be there for her. I wish I could take away her pain. My chest constricts, and it feels as though someone is stepping on it, making it hard to breathe.

I grab my black leather journal that's worn around the edges, flicking through the pages that are covered in ink. Words that hold my deepest and darkest thoughts. I laugh. It knows me better than anyone.

I grip the black pen and start writing. With every stroke of ink, the heaviness on my chest starts to dissipate.

I feel trapped. Like I'm detained in my own home. With my hands gripping the bars. I'm screaming. Let me out. I feel helpless. Useless. I want to help, to make a difference and have some kind of purpose in this world.

I'm sick of being the precious princess who's locked in her tower. I want to do something useful. To have some kind of impact. All I do is shop. Party. Sleep with men who are too scared of my brother to fuck me right. It's fun, but it doesn't mean anything to me anymore.

I've tried to do more in The Brotherhood, but Gage doesn't allow it. He doesn't want me to be part of it, says it's his job, his responsibility, and no girl should be put in the firing line. He doesn't want me getting hurt. He'd never forgive himself if I did. But can't he see I'm fading away here? That doing nothing is slowly killing me?

I wish he'd notice or listen to me. Give me some kind of responsibility. But as a woman in this man's world, I know I stand a snowball's chance in hell.

I hate that it's this way.

What would it be like if women were in power instead? Like me in charge of The Brotherhood. I know it'd never happen, but I can dream here. Of a time when I'm in charge of a movement to create union. Where women have more of a voice.

There's a knock on my door. I finish the last line.

And I will.

I close my book, then put it into my top drawer. After rolling off my bed, I push my feet into my slippers and make my way over. Opening the door, I'm met with a familiar set of brown eyes. Lily, my old nanny. Huh? What's she doing here? Still, one look at those familiar eyes, and I notice the sheen of tears.

My arms fly around her neck, and I pull her in. Her rosy scent feels like a warm hug.

"Oh, I've missed you," I say, and Lily wails, holding me tighter. Oh God—something must be seriously wrong.

As wetness soaks into my knitted top, I pull back. Tears line her wrinkled cheeks, and I bring her into my room, closing the door.

"I'm so glad they let you in," I say, and Lily wipes away her tears. "Are you okay?" I ask the question, though I already know she's not.

I study her closely. Her graying hair is a mess, with pieces falling all around her face. Her eyes are bloodshot, and tears spill from them effortlessly. My heart aches as I wait for her to answer.

"I need your help." Her words come out hoarse. She takes a seat on my bed, and I join her, taking her small hand in mine.

"Anything." I mean it—I'd do anything for her.

She's looked after me for as long as I can remember. It broke my heart when she left the family three years ago when I turned eighteen. Gage had insisted it was time for her to leave, but I hadn't wanted her to. It was silly, a grown girl needing her nanny still, but it was nice to have a woman around—someone I could talk to about all the crazy things in my life. She never judged me, just always listened.

"It's Jewel," Lily says, and my chest tightens.

When Lily was fired, I lost my friend too. Jewel and I said we'd keep in touch, but she never returned my calls, and as time went on, I stopped making them. Maybe she was eager to get away from The Brotherhood princess, just like everyone else seems to be.

Still, I care for her.

"What about her?" I ask, tensing up.

"She's missing," Lily sobs.

"What do you mean, missing?"

Lily releases my hand and wipes hers on her linen pants. "I haven't seen her much in three years, since we stopped working here." Her words hang heavily in my room.

"What happened?" I ask, and Lily looks out the open door to my balcony.

"She began coming home late, with more money too. She was working at a restaurant called Pini. Then she started changing, becoming more distant. Never coming home, spending her nights with her 'new friends,' as she called them." Lily releases a heavy breath.

That doesn't sound like my old friend. She always loved being with Lily; she adored her mother.

"I should have tried harder to ask if she was okay when I did see her, but I didn't. We always fought. She wouldn't tell me what was going on."

Lily hangs her head in her hands.

"She's sent text messages, but they have gotten less frequent, and something feels off. Please help me. I've gone to the police, but they haven't found anything, and I don't know what else to do. You're my only hope. Could you ask around The Brotherhood? Talk to your brother? If anyone can find out where she is, it's them."

Lily looks at me, and I kneel down in front of her, taking her hands in mine. Tears stain her cheeks, and my heart aches for her. For Jewel.

"Do you know who her new friends are? Does she have a boyfriend?" I ask.

Lily shakes her head. "I don't know. I should have asked, but I didn't."

"When did you last hear from her?"

"The last message was about two months ago," Lily says.

"Show me."

She releases my hands and takes her phone from her pocket, tapping the screen a couple of times before passing it to me. I lean back on my heels, scrolling through pages of unanswered messages from Lily. When I find the old messages from Jewel, they are short and to the point.

Miss you.

I'm okay.

Can't see you, just have a lot going on with work at the moment. Everything is fine. I'm happy.

They go on and on, the most recent messages even shorter than the ones that came before. The last one is dated August 18th—two months ago. It's a photo of Jewel. Her long, bright-red hair stands out, and I remember being jealous of it as a kid. I wanted to dye my hair so we could be twins. Her brown eyes look dull, the sparkle gone. Her smile looks forced, and something just feels off about the photo.

"That's the last one I got. I've been trying to call her every day since, and now her phone is off." Lily's voice crumbles, and my heart breaks for her. Not knowing where your daughter is must be the worst kind of pain.

I stare at the photo, my fingers hovering over her beautiful face. There's a logo in the background on the wall. I zoom in. It's blurry, but I can identify half the blue letters—IGHT—and some thick lines.

Something about it looks familiar, but I have no idea where I might have seen it or what it is.

"Can I send myself this photo?"

Lily nods, her hands shaking in her lap.

"I'll do whatever it takes to find her, Lily. I promise." I don't break eye contact with her, and her throat bobs. As more tears stain her cheeks, I want to take away all her pain.

Lily looked after me when I needed her most, so I'm going to do the same for her. I'll bring Jewel home and heal her pain.

"Do you know of any other girls who've been taken or missing?" I ask.

Lily frowns. "Well, yeah, people go missing all the time, especially in Daringhood, but no one ever does anything about it."

It feels like someone punched me in the gut.

No one ever does anything about it. I want to help, to do something for them. To find them and bring them home or somewhere safe.

My brother has always had The Brotherhood as his purpose, and now I've found something that I can do to make a positive change and help save Jewel.

CHAPTER SEVEN

K ^{ai}

The Brotherhood can shove their fancy cars up their asses.

I pinch my black onyx crystal around my neck with my fingers, praying it'll give me the strength I need to keep my shit together. But I fucking doubt it.

Zion whistles, opening the door to the Rimac Nevera R that's worth more than all the cars in Daringhood put together. Two cars sit on our side of the train tracks, with a note stuck to one of the windshields. I take it, reading over the black ink.

They're not your guns, but they're something. Let's meet. —Gage

Of course, they didn't deliver the guns Dominic owed us. Fucking assholes. Once more, the Daringville rich pricks have screwed us over because we're from the wrong side of the tracks.

Scrunching the note up, I flick my lighter. Flames dance into the night, and the note vanishes into ash.

I should light the cars on fire, too, as a sign that we don't want their attempted peace offering. They've already made their bed, and they'll lie in it.

Fuck them and Freya, the woman who left Daringhood for the men who lead Daringville. My heart skips a beat. I'll never truly hate her—she'll always be my best friend—but she chose them over me, and that hurts more than I'd ever admit out loud. We were both there for each other during a time when no one else was. She's family.

"It's something," Zion mumbles, opening the door and running his hand over the steering wheel.

"Bear would love these," he says.

I nod. "But fuck them and their shit offerings. We want our weapons."

"You might not want their handouts, but we need the money." Zion pauses, scratching the back of his head. "I need this money to build a place for my daughter."

Guilt punches me in the gut, and I nod.

"Message Joey to take them to his garage and put them up for auction. I'm sure someone from Daringville or the surrounding towns will want them."

I start walking away, lighting up a joint. The smoke fills my lungs, but it does fuck all to relax my tense shoulders. We can use this money to buy the weapons we were owed. To build our army and take more power from them—The Brotherhood.

Zion falls into step with me; he doesn't say anything. A man of few words. Being around him is easy. He doesn't fill every second with noise just because. Most people hate the silence, scared of hearing their own thoughts. Always planning what to say next, what to ask. With Zion, he only says what he needs to—nothing more, nothing less.

"Where's Bear?" I ask, taking another drag and passing it to Zion.

He points up the road to one of the old train station buildings, the one we left Bear and Lucas in hours ago. I thought Bear would be done with The Brotherhood leader by now, but maybe not.

When we get there, the door to the station is half open. Zion kicks it in. The loud bang of the wood hitting the wall echoes through the quiet space. I follow him inside and into a dark, open room. Chairs line the walls, half ripped up and sitting sideways or completely broken.

No one's here, but there's fresh blood on the ground. Hopefully Lucas's and not Bear's. Where the fuck is he?

After shoving my hand into my pocket, I grab my phone and hit dial on his number. It rings out. Fuck.

When Bear's missing, there's trouble. He's one of my closest friends, but he's unpredictable—never going along with a plan, always fucking it up and doing whatever he chooses. It makes him a liability, and it grinds on my last nerve. I need to know everything—every last detail. Bear knows this but still defies me.

We head back outside and start walking toward the trailer park. I bring the last of the joint to my lips, even though it's done fuck all to relax me. I throw it to the ground, then shove my hands into the pockets of my leather jacket.

Zion sucks in a breath and points past the trailer park to the amusement park. Red-and-white lights beam into the sky, and I curse. If Bear is at his park and the lights are on, he's entertaining someone, and who knows what condition they'll be in by the time we get there?

Ten minutes later, we reach the entrance to the park. That stupid fucking clown stares right through me, sending a shiver down my back. Fucking hate clowns. Bear is obsessed with his playground. When he found it when we were like thirteen, he fell in love and claimed it as his.

He's lived here ever since, restoring the rooms and making it his playhouse. I hate coming here. Everything is messy, unorganized, and unpredictable—three things I hate most in this world. It fits Bear perfectly.

Zion opens the latch to the back of the building next to the clown and disappears down the stairs. I pull the door shut behind me and descend the dark stairs as well. The metal creaks under my feet with each step. At the bottom, Zion parts the red-velvet curtain, and we move through.

A large L-shaped couch sits in the middle of the room. The walls are covered in graffiti and mirrors. Bear and his mirrors. The bright-red carpet burns my eyes. It's different, but nothing like the rest of his playground, which I refuse to go through. Once is enough; I'll never walk through that horror show again. Not if I don't have to.

"Can you go find him and bring him back here?" I fall back onto the couch, and Zion disappears through the curtain again.

I run my fingers through my hair. What the fuck do we do now? It's time to take action against The Brotherhood. We've waited long enough, but the new leaders—they're weak. I'm done playing games.

They took someone from me a long time ago, and I've been waiting for my time to avenge her. We never stood a chance, but now—with the young boys at the helm and Lucas in custody—maybe we do. War is coming to their doorstep, and I won't stop until I have my revenge.

We needed those guns from Dominic, but now that he's dead, there's no way Gage, Hazen, or Lucas will hand them over. Why would they give us more power to use against them? That's just fucking stupid. Probably why they gave us those cars.

They blew up the fucking town hall, killing all those men. We had a deal with Dominic—more guns would give us more strength to take them down.

How can we bring them down now without the weapons? We can't. We need weapons and an army. I'm done with The Brotherhood ruling over our town.

We need to build up our own army to fight them. To take over. There are some guys I trust—about ten or so in our 18hood rap crew. Another twenty from the trailer park down the street. A handful of good dudes from work at the meat-packing factory.

I sit in silence for at least ten minutes.

The curtain opens and Zion waves me over, his eyebrows drawn together and anger clear in his eyes. Fucking hell. What has Bear done?

Without a second thought, I follow Zion out. He opens a door leading into another room of mirrors. Sweat forms on my forehead and drips down my cheeks. I see my reflection everywhere I look, my dark-brown eyes staring right through me. Fuck this place.

The next room is full of butterflies. The hot, steamy air clings to my skin. Being in here isn't so bad. It's calming. Blue, red, and purple butterflies fly around me. They are pretty. The air shifts as we move through another door. The roof is open, and the dark, starry night glares back at me.

Rows and rows of coffins line the dirt, all old, cracked, and covered in cobwebs. Skulls and bones line some of the surfaces and look like they are staring right through me. Why can't Bear live in a normal fucking house instead of this? Bear buries all his victims here, and I've lost count of how many people he's killed. Some he clearly doesn't even bother to bury, just leaving them on top of the graves. It smells like death. I cover my nose, trying to fight off the urge to vomit. I shake my head, moving into the next room, and all the air is sucked from my lungs.

There's a girl strapped to a spinning target, her black, wavy hair covering half of her face.

Her green eyes look up, pleading with me to save her, and all I can see is my sister. I reach for Zion, clutching his shoulder. My heart squeezes.

The ground below me falls through, taking me into the depths of hell.

Chapter Eight

A^{mirah}

After I passed out, I woke up strapped to some kind of target. The room spins around and around. Everything becomes blurry, merging. I squeeze my eyes shut and my stomach falls beneath me. I'm going to be sick. I'm jerked to a stop, but my head feels like I'm still spinning. Like I'm on one of those rides at an amusement park, except this one isn't stopping, and it's not fun. It's torture.

My hands and legs are spread out, bound to a large, oversized target, the kind you'd find on a dartboard—and my chest is the bullseye. The rope digs into my skin, burning my flesh with every movement. Bear grins at me from the other side of the room, his eyes alight, his hand still on the lever that I've come to learn will send me spinning.

I take several fast breaths in and out. It takes me a second to calm down.

The door creaks open, then slams shut. Zion, another of Kai's friends I've seen around the tracks a few times, stops just inside the door, staring at me with a blank expression.

Behind him, a familiar pair of dark-brown eyes meets mine. They belong to Kai, a guy I barely know but who my best friend trusts implicitly. They are wide at first, then turn to slits.

"What the fuck?" Kai growls, and I glance between him, Zion, and Bear, watching them closely. Taking in everything they do and say. My brother taught me to always be on alert, know where the exits are, and understand every situation.

Bear's hand is wrapped around the lever, ready to pull at any second. He's smiling and totally ignores Kai.

Zion watches me closely, his brows drawn in slightly, his head cocked to the side. He doesn't move his gaze from my face, and I feel like he's looking into my psyche. In the handful of moments I've seen him, he's always been quiet. There's something about him that feels safe, like he wouldn't hurt me.

I lick my dry lips and mouth the word *help*.

The corner of his mouth twitches ever so slightly, and for a second, I think I've imagined it. My head feels fuzzy, still spinning. He looks away, and my stomach drops. He's not going to save me.

"Bear?" Kai's voice turns deep.

"Oh, have you met the princess of The Brotherhood? This is Amirah," Bear says, waving his hand my way.

Kai shakes his head. "I know who the fuck she is. I didn't ask that. I meant, what is she doing here?"

"She's your birthday present. I know I'm early, but you'll forgive me?" Bear pushes out his bottom lip, and I fight the urge to throw up. Bile sits in the pit of my stomach, threatening to release. Preferably all over Bear.

"I don't want a spoiled Brotherhood princess for my birthday, you idiot. Let her go." Kai takes a step toward me, and the bile turns into what feels like a flutter of hope in my belly. He's going to let me go?

I have no idea how long I've been here. Time stopped the second I woke up in this hellhole. If I spend another minute here, I'm going to go crazy, end up like Bear. Hell, the way I acted on that roller coaster with him, allowing him to get me off? Who the fuck even am I?

"I thought you'd be proud of me," Bear says, frowning at Kai.

Kai shakes his head. "You thought wrong."

Bear's gaze breaks, and he stares at his feet, his cheeks turning a light shade of pink. He looks genuinely hurt.

Kai stands in front of me, the smell of weed clinging to the air around us. He reaches out, and I suck in a deep breath, squeezing my eyes shut, waiting for the impact. But it never comes. I open my eyes to find his tattooed hand gripping my chin softly. His intense brown eyes soften ever so slightly, turning to a lighter shade. He stares at me for several heartbeats, and I forget where we are and what we're doing.

He's Freya's best friend. He wouldn't hurt me, because that would mean hurting her, and he'd never do that.

As I lick my dry lips, he watches the movement closely. His thumb runs over my bottom lip, and it feels like I'm spinning again. My pulse quickens. My legs and arms are spread apart, allowing him access to every part of me. I'm vulnerable and at his mercy. It's easy to forget for a moment that my life is on the line.

I force myself to turn my head away. I have to. He's the enemy, and I won't be drawn into his darkness. I'm their captive, not their friend—or whatever the hell that was between us.

"Enough!" Bear yells, and Kai steps back, raising his hands.

The air around us returns to normal, and I suck in several breaths.

"Take her home," Kai demands.

Bear chuckles. "Not going to happen. She's not going anywhere." He winks at me, and I squeeze my hands into fists.

"What's your plan then?" Kai asks.

Zion stays quiet, eyes darting between his friends and occasionally back to me.

"Let me guess—The Brotherhood didn't deliver the guns," Bear says, completely ignoring Kai's question.

"Just a couple of cars."

Bear's eyes light up for a moment, then they flicker back to me. "So we don't have what we need to take them on now. If we want power over The Brotherhood, we need leverage. May I introduce you to Miss Leverage, Amirah Ledger!" Bear presses a button, and a round of canned applause sounds from the speakers. His mouth lifts, his eyes sparkling. This is all just a big game to him. I'm his doll, someone to play with until I break.

"The idea of taking Freya is one thing. She knows us, she trusts us, but you have a woman here who doesn't, and she's petrified in this creepy-as-fuck place." Kai speaks as if I'm not in the room, his attention focused on Bear. I feel like I'm part of a private conversation, one I shouldn't be witness to. Kai doesn't want me here—that's one thing I'm sure of and something I can use to my advantage.

"Who cares? Freya would be safe, yes, but having someone this close to them gives us an advantage. We'd be pulling the strings," Zion says, and his words are sharp and smooth, like a knife that's been dipped in honey. It's the first time I've heard him speak, and I didn't expect him to be on board with Bear. The kindness in his eyes that I thought I saw earlier? I must have imagined it.

"What are you saying? We hold her hostage for money?" Kai scoffs. "They'll never give us guns—look how well that worked out last time."

Zion crosses his arms over his chest. "So we pump her for intel. Use her."

"Like she'd know anything. She's just a princess."

"Princesses see things they shouldn't." Bear winks at me, and I glare back.

"Fine, say she does know something. How do we get that information from her? By torture?" Kai looks my way, his gaze running slowly over my body. My breathing quickens, and I want to scream at him, but no words come out.

"By whatever fucking means necessary," Zion snaps, and I'm acutely aware of my vulnerable state—strapped to a board—once more.

"How would you feel if she was your daughter?" Kai glances back at Zion, and his face turns an angry shade of red.

He moves like lightning, getting right up in Kai's face, and Bear jumps into action. Zion grips Kai's jacket, and Bear stands close to them, watching it all unfold. I need to move now, while they're distracted.

I reach for the rope, tugging at the end piece. This might be my only chance to escape, and I won't waste it.

CHAPTER NINE

Z ion

Grabbing the collar of Kai's leather jacket, I stare into his dark-brown eyes. How fucking dare he mention my daughter, asking how I'd feel if Amirah was her? Revealing that I have a kid to one of our enemies—the princess of The Brotherhood, no less. No one is supposed to know about her, especially since she's currently living on enemy fucking territory.

If my daughter was in Amirah's shoes, I would have blown the whole fucking town to the ground to get her back. She's the only reason I'm still breathing. She's my savior, and now more than ever, I can't allow anything to get in the way of seeing her. It's already hard enough.

"What the fuck?!" I growl right in his face.

Kai doesn't flinch. He holds his hands up in surrender. "I just want you to know what's at stake here."

I scoff, shoving him backward, and he stumbles before righting himself. "Amirah knows about her now, so she's not going anywhere."

Realization slams into Kai, his jaw twitching. "Fuck. Sorry, bro."

Kai had to mention her in front of Amirah. Now she knows, and that cuts deeper than a knife. No one apart from us knows about her. I don't know Amirah or trust her. She's our enemy, and now she knows my best-kept secret.

I storm out the door, moving through every fucked-up room until I'm back in the living room and falling onto the couch. It doesn't take long for the door to open and the curtain to swish open and closed.

"I'm sorry. I fucked up," Kai says. The couch dips beside me.

I don't reply, because what's the fucking point? He knows how I feel about what he did. I'm not going to waste words. My daughter is a secret, and hell, she doesn't even know I'm her father. That's how it's had to be until recently. Now everything has changed.

I didn't want her getting caught up in our shit or this town, but I have no fucking clue what to do. Everything could be ruined if Amirah gets out and tells The Brotherhood about Cleo. If they ever found her, they could use her against us, just like we are doing with Amirah.

I might be on board with using Amirah to our advantage, but taking her in the first place was a fucking stupid idea. Still, that's Bear—if he gets an idea in his head, nothing will stop him. Now that she's here, she isn't leaving. I won't allow it. Not until Cleo is safe.

The door slams shut, and Bear struts in, heading straight for the fridge in the corner of the room, where he grabs a can of beer. He opens it and finishes it in three mouthfuls, then throws the can into the trash bin next to the fridge.

"Kidnapping is exhausting." He sighs, sitting down on the opposite side of me.

I scoff, folding my hands behind my head.

"They're going to come for us soon. What's your grand plan?" Kai asks, leaning back against the cushion.

"Haven't thought that far ahead." Bear yawns, covering his mouth with his hand. "Maybe I'll say we'll take her instead of the cars."

I roll my eyes. Of course he fucking hasn't. Bear takes action without thinking of the consequences first.

"We need to go after them before they come for us. We've held off before because Dom's been too strong, then Freya was in the crossfire. Now there are holes in their leadership. They have newbies they've recruited. It's the perfect time to strike," Kai says.

I ponder Kai's words for several heartbeats. He's right, and it would be stupid for us to sit around and do nothing. All I've ever wanted is a safe place to raise my daughter—one where we are free to do as we please. A life where I have enough money to provide her with everything she needs to grow.

I release my hands and reach into my pocket. After pulling out my lighter, I flick the ignition. A small flame dances in front of me. It's strong, fearless, but I have control. I let go and the light disappears. Flicking it back on again, I run it under my arm. My skin starts to burn. The fight within me is strong. My skin starts to become unbearably hot.

"What are you proposing we do?" I ask, releasing the flame and a heavy exhale. My skin burns, a reminder that I'm in control.

"Take down The Brotherhood, remove the divide, and hit them where it hurts." Kai's eyes turn dark, and he starts to bounce his knee up and down.

"And how does that look, exactly?" I ask.

"We need to build an army bigger than theirs and have enough weapons to use against them. I'm done working my ass off for nothing. Living like this," Kai says, leaving out the truth behind it all.

He wants revenge for his sister, and that's something I understand. Like his need to protect Freya—it's all because he couldn't save his sister.

"What about Freya?" I ask.

"What about her?" Kai says, sitting up straighter.

"Would you tie her to a target board if you had to?" Bear asks with a grin.

I roll my eyes. "Bear, get a new fucking hobby. No, Kai—I just mean she might ask you to stop again. She's one of them now. She chose them. And what will you do if she does?" I ask the hard question because, fuck, it's one of Kai's downfalls. He'd still move mountains for Freya. She was his best friend. I get it. I'd do anything for my brothers, too, but he has to choose us over her now.

Kai runs his hands through his short hair, messing it up before he pins me with a heavy stare. "I'll do what needs to be done."

I like Freya. She was once one of us, but now she's sleeping with the enemy, and we can't afford to let her be our downfall.

"We need more people on our side," I say. "And we need weapons."

There's a light thump against the door we came through, but Bear and Kai don't notice it. I watch the red curtains closely for several seconds, but nothing happens. Maybe it was the wind.

"We need a nuke, so I can just blow them all up." Bear grins even wider, and I shake my head.

"What?" I scoff. "Then we die anyway from radiation?"

His mouth falls open and he curses. "I can get us more money to get weapons from someone else."

"How?"

The corner of Bear's mouth raises. "The usual—people pay for these guns of steel." He flexes his muscles, and I roll my eyes.

"We need more than funds and men to take down The Brotherhood," I say. "We need to play this smart. We need to figure out how many of their men are left after the blowup with Dominic, and where their weapons are. Find out more about the docks, their shipments—if we can take over that, we can control the whole district."

"What about using women for intel?" Bear suggests. "I mean, we've got the perfect starting point with Amirah at our disposal."

I open my mouth to tell him to shut up, but maybe he has a point.

"Why women? Everyone knows The Brotherhood is a male-run organization," Kai says.

"No, Bear's onto something. Those boys are pussy-whipped by Freya; she's basically got a seat at the table. Could be that this is a new age of The Brotherhood, where the women have more voice, and there's nothing a woman loves more than a bleeding-heart sob story."

All the men in the ville are loyal to The Brotherhood, but perhaps the women could be persuaded to join us.

Kai throws his phone at Bear, and he catches it.

"Get one of your friends at the club to run interference for us. Tell them that you heard Amirah was taken by some college guys in Berkeley. It'll give us time to figure this shit out," Kai says, and Bear breathes out heavily through his nose.

"I'll see what I can do."

I feel eyes on me. I sit up straight, glancing over my shoulder toward the curtains. They're open, just a crack. I hit Bear on his leg, pointing toward the doorway, and all hell breaks loose.

CHAPTER TEN

B efore
   Amirah

I watch Gage from across the dinner table as he takes one, then two bites of his pasta. The corner of his mouth lifts.

"This is good, Amirah. When you insisted on helping the chef, I thought you'd ruin it, but you've surprised me," he says with a laugh.

Jerk. A simple thanks would have been nice.

I ignore him, rolling the pasta around with my fork, and stare off into space. Jewel is all I've been able to think about since Lily came over this morning.

I've called around to a few of our neighbors to see if any of them have young girls working for them as maids, but they don't. I went downtown, showing people her photo, and even went down to the tracks, but it led to no answers. I searched the internet for any information about her and the letters from the photo, but again, nothing came up.

Is she okay? Where is she? It doesn't matter that I haven't heard from or seen her in years. I'd hate it if something happened to her.

"Spit it out," Gage says from across the kitchen table.

"That obvious something's up, hey?"

"Sis, you have zero poker face." He grins, and I sigh.

"You remember Jewel?"

"How could I forget? You were joined at the hip with her."

"Lily came over yesterday and said Jewel is missing."

Gage takes a sip of his drink, then places it back down on the table. "Yeah, and?"

I drop the fork, and it clinks against the bowl. "Are you fucking serious?"

"What do you want, Amirah? Use your fucking words," Gage snaps, and I bite into my bottom lip, anger swirling up inside of me.

"God, you're such a fucking asshole. I don't know how Freya puts up with you."

Gage snorts, but I ignore him.

"Lily thinks there's something more to it. How could I find her? Can you help me, or can someone from The Brotherhood?"

He sighs. "We've got enough shit going on, Amirah. A war is brewing, and if we don't figure it out, people won't just go missing. They'll be dead. *That's* my priority. I can't help you with this." Gage pushes back his chair and moves around the table.

I grab his arm, and he stops. "But where should I start?" I ask, pleading with him to give me something, anything. I've never done anything like this before, and I want to help. I want to bring Jewel home—for Lily.

"You need to look at the last communication she had with her mother." Gage pulls out of my grip and sighs again. "But, Amirah, fair warning—she probably just ran off, and you're wasting your time."

"I've got nothing better to do," I say, pushing away my pasta before standing and then heading toward the door.

"There have been rumors of a few women going missing. Could be something going on. Not here but in the Hood."

I pull out my phone, bringing up the last photo Lily received of Jewel, and flashing it in front of Gage. "Does this look familiar to you?"

He brushes past me. "I don't have time to play detective. Just drop it, Amirah. I don't want you caught up in this or going anywhere near the Hood with the state of things between them and us." Gage leaves and I curse.

There's no way in hell I'm dropping this. Lily came to me because she trusts me. She needs me, and I'm done with being locked in my bedroom by my brother, who clearly just expects me to play house. Freya is grieving her brother and forging a new life with her men. All my other friends are waiting around to be wives. I want a purpose, and finding Jewel is it.

CHAPTER ELEVEN

Amirah

I bite down on the rope, tugging. It doesn't budge much. *Fuck*. I release it, spitting out the fibers stuck to my tongue. Pulling down, I try to make my hand as small as it can be. If I can release one hand, then I can free myself from these constraints. Kai, Zion, and Bear are gone—this might be my only chance to escape, and I won't waste it.

My arms and legs feel weak from being pinned to the target. Every muscle aches. I keep pulling. Blood drips down my fingers. The rope burns my skin, but I can't stop. My hand moves along the rope, just slightly, and hope blooms inside me. A couple more inches, then I'm free—well, at least one hand will be.

Sweat runs down my forehead and into my eyes. I squeeze them shut, gritting my teeth. I want to be home, sleeping in my own bed, talking this whole wild ordeal over with Freya. Does Gage know I'm gone? By now, surely they have The Brotherhood out looking for me.

It won't be long until they're knocking down Bear's door. Do theme parks have a door? I wouldn't know since I was unconscious when I was dragged in. Then this will all be put behind me and I can go back to my life. Away from this hell.

My hand releases, falling to my side. I grin, opening my eyes, and get to work untying my other hand, then my legs. I drop to the ground, and my legs give way. I fall onto my knees, pain biting into my skin as I brace my hands on the concrete floor. Blood covers my right hand, both from the rope burn and my attempt at self-defense with the mirror, turning my stomach.

Move.

As I push myself back up, my head spins and the room blurs before the concrete comes back to me. I stand, my feet wobbling. Multiple targets and other carnival games fill the room. Clowns with open mouths move from left to right, and bottles hang from the ceiling. Where's the door? I don't remember coming into the room; my memory is fuzzy. I move toward the wall, reaching out, and I brush along the white paint.

I follow the wall until my fingers wrap around the doorknob. I twist and it opens. As I peer through the tiny gap, darkness meets me. Kai, Zion, and Bear aren't in here. I step onto the dirt-covered floor. The roof is gone, and the dark, star-filled sky meets me. A half-moon gives me the slightest bit of light.

There are rows and rows of coffins. Skulls lie on top of some, and it feels like they are staring right through me. The dead don't scare me. I've seen so much death in my life that it barely even registers. They can't hurt me anymore. It's the living that do.

The next room is hot, sticky, and filled with butterflies. The fluttering of their wings sounds like a lullaby. They calm me, and my shoulders relax for the first time tonight. A large yellow-and-orange butterfly lands on my forearm, then another and another. The downlights reflect off their wings. I move quickly through the room toward the next door, and by the time I get there, I'm covered in butterflies. Maybe they can lift me out of here. I scoff to myself. Yeah, not going to happen.

Some of the butterflies stay with me as I step into the room full of mirrors. My reflection is everywhere, following me around. My brown hair sticks to my skin, and my face is a ghoulish white and black from my mascara running down my cheeks. I look like a mess.

Voices carry through from the next room. I reach the door and open it slightly, peering inside. I'm met with a deep-red curtain. I step forward, peeking through the little gap. Kai, Zion, and Bear are sitting on a large couch, with their backs to the door, in deep conversation. The room is covered in graffiti and mirrors.

"We need more people on our side," Zion says. "And we need weapons."

More people? Are they going to take more women like me?

I suck in a breath, then quickly cover my mouth.

My elbow hits the wall. I quickly shut the curtain, taking a step back. My pulse speeds up, my chest rising and falling as I wait for them to come through the red velvet, but after several heartbeats, no one comes.

I can't go in there—not with them sitting around in wait—but I can't return the way I came from either. It only leads back to the room where I was trapped.

I open the curtain once again, peering back inside. They are still sitting on the couch.

"We need a nuke, so I can just blow them all up," Bear says, grinning.

I swallow past the lump in my throat. After being with Bear tonight, it wouldn't surprise me if he did find a way to get a weapon of mass destruction. We'd all be dead, gone in seconds.

"What? Then we die anyway from radiation?" Zion asks, taking the words from my own mouth.

Bear's mouth falls open, and he curses. "I can get us more money to get weapons from someone else."

"How?" Zion asks, and the corner of Bear's mouth raises.

"The usual—people pay for these guns of steel," he flexes his muscles, and Zion rolls his eyes.

"We need more than funds and men to take down The Brotherhood," Zion says. "We need to play this smart. We need to figure out how many of their men are left after the blowup with Dominic, and where their weapons are. Maybe find out more about the docks, their shipments—if we can take over that, we can control the whole district."

"What about using women for intel?" Bear suggests. "I mean, we've got the perfect starting point with Amirah at our disposal."

"Why women? Everyone knows The Brotherhood is a male-run organization," Kai says.

"No, Bear's onto something. Those boys are pussy-whipped by Freya; she's basically got a seat at the table. Maybe this is a new age of The Brotherhood, where the women have more voice, and there's nothing a woman loves more than a bleeding-heart sob story," Zion says.

Kai throws his phone at Bear, and he catches it.

"Get one of your friends at the club to run interference for us. Tell them that you heard Amirah was taken by some college guys in

Berkeley. It'll give us time to figure this shit out," Kai says, and Bear breathes out heavily through his nose.

"I'll see what I can do," Bear says.

I swallow hard. I want to scream, to run, but I can't move. They have it all wrong. Women hold so much more power than they realize. If they went about this differently, if they knew that, they could gain the upper hand against The Brotherhood.

The women in the ville—or at least this woman—are done with being treated like second-class citizens just because they have a pussy. I've heard the talk at parties and around town. Women are over being told "not to worry." The town hall was blown up! We're allowed to be concerned. And after what I've discovered these last few months, with everything that happened with Jewel . . . we're ready to fight back.

The Brotherhood focuses on the men having the power, but what they don't realize is that behind each man at the table there's a powerful woman. I think they are scared of that; they don't want to give us too much, because they know when a woman is in her full power, she's the true leader. If we weren't, how else would Freya have been able to make the three most obstinate men I've met fall to their knees?

Before I can take my next breath, the curtain is ripped open in front of me.

"Boo!" Bear grins, and I scream, taking one, then two steps back through the door and into the room of mirrors.

I run, but everywhere I look, I'm met with myself, and Bear is behind me. His bright-blond hair follows as I run, screaming my lungs out until my throat is dry.

A hand lands on my shoulder, spinning me around, and then I'm forced backward. My back slams into one of the mirrors. A crack pierces my ears. He pushes into me. I feel every inch of his body against mine, his hard cock and bulging muscles pinning me to the mirror.

He takes my jaw, turning my head, but I refuse to look at him. "Fuck, baby. I want to bottle up your screams and listen to them while I stroke my cock."

He leans in, his breath hot against my cheek. When he swipes his tongue over my skin, my body reacts. A million butterflies flutter around in my stomach, my skin burns hot, and I squeeze my eyes shut. I don't understand why my body is responding this way. He's a bad person. I'm trapped here because of him. I hate him, but apparently my body is on the fence.

"Enlighten me, princess. What's going on in that pretty head of yours?"

"Bear, leave her alone," Kai says from somewhere in the dark room.

Bear moves his fingers along my throat, between my neck and ear. I feel the *thump thump* of my pulse against his touch. He wraps his fingers around my crystal necklace and tugs, cutting off the air to my lungs. I want to scream.

"You feel that?" he whispers, his hot breath tickling my ear. I shake my head, and Bear chuckles, then releases the necklace. I gasp for air. "You are my favorite captive yet, and I've only had you for a couple of hours. There's so much more fun to be had, my princess."

I force open my eyes, glaring into his bright-green irises, and roll my shoulders back. "Fuck you. I'm no one's captive, and I won't be here much longer."

Bear laughs. "We'll see about that. Keep on fighting me, princess. It makes it so much more fun."

"Enough!" Kai yells. His reflection bounces off the mirrors, and he watches me with a mixture of pain and hatred. "Take her and put her somewhere safe."

Bear steps away, and my back sags against the mirror. My breathing evens back out, and I look between Bear, Kai, and the open door. I could try to run for it, but I'm not going to get far if I do—and I presume Zion is still on the other side of that door, anyway.

Bear reaches for me, and I move out of his way. Glass pierces my bare feet. Ouch. The corner of his mouth lifts before he pounces, gripping my forearm, then he pulls me out of the room and back into the living room.

Zion is gone, and Kai exits through another door, leaving it open behind him. The cool night air whips through the space, kissing my cheeks. An exit.

I stare at the empty doorway longingly. If I can break free from Bear's hold and run, I'll make it outside.

With all the strength I have left, I slam my foot down on Bear's, and he growls, releasing my arm slightly, which gives me enough momentum to break free.

I run without looking back toward the open door.

Freedom, here I come.

Chapter Twelve

B ear

She's not getting away from me. From us. She's only been here a couple of hours, and I'm already hooked.

She isn't like anyone else I've ever met. There's a fire in her eyes, waiting to explode. Begging to be released. She isn't fit to be a princess of The Brotherhood, protected and hidden away in her castle. Fuck, no. Amirah Ledger is a queen, a leader. I can feel it. She has so much power just waiting to be pulled from within her, and I'm going to help her. Help her see that and step into her power. By testing her limits. By challenging her until she's at breaking point, then watching as she rises from the ashes.

Her long black hair blows behind her shoulders as she runs through the living room, straight toward the open door. Fucking Kai. Why would he leave it open?

Because he wants her to leave. He wants to give her an option. He's fucking weak when it comes to women. Freya's always been his downfall, and now he's helping Amirah.

I'll give her to the count of ten once she's out of sight. My breathing picks up.

Don't let her leave. Get her.

I will. Wait. Seven, eight, nine, and ten.

I move at speed up the stairs. The cool night air is a welcome relief. The lights from my amusement park make it easy for me to spot her running on the dirt path along the line of my park, past the roller coasters, her long hair moving with the wind. I sprint after her, getting closer and closer. She glances over her shoulder, her gaze catching mine. The skin between her eyebrows pinches and her eyes widen.

She pushes her legs faster and harder, but she's not as quick as me. I turn, moving behind one of the roller coasters. She doesn't know this place like I do. She'll think she's free, that I'm gone, and that's how I like it. I want her to feel that excitement building inside her. To believe she's nearly out of here for good.

Her heavy breathing sounds close as I reach the end of the roller coaster, stand in the shadow of the control booth, and wait. *Five, four, three, two, and one.*

I jump out and she screams. Covering her mouth with my hand, I pull her back against me. She thrashes against my hold, her elbows hitting into my stomach, but I don't dare let her go. After a minute, her body deflates and she gives in, as if now she knows her fate.

My finger reaches her pulse on her wrist, and it thumps percussively, just like someone playing the drums. I release my hand covering her mouth, and she sucks in a couple of deep breaths.

I pull her back around the roller coaster, heading straight for the slide.

As I shove Amirah onto the faded yellow slide, she doesn't fight me. She knows she can't escape—at least, not tonight. I can imagine that flame still burning beneath her eyes, and I don't ever want that to disappear. I want it to grow brighter, and I'm going to have fun playing with her, bringing out the best of her.

"Time for our beauty sleep, princess." I press a sloppy kiss against her cheek before shoving her forward. A small gasp leaves her throat as she disappears down the tube, and I follow her.

Darkness consumes me, and I'd love to curl up in here to sleep. It feels safe, like a warm blanket surrounding me. Like nothing can touch me here as I catapult through the tunnel.

All too soon, I reach the end. Amirah isn't anywhere to be seen. I brace my hands on the slide and push out. The small room is dark—I can't see her. After grabbing my phone, I switch on the light. There in the corner is Amirah, curled up in a ball. Her arms are wrapped around her knees, her brows drawn in, and her plump lips are pulled back in a snarl. I smile.

"You okay, little princess?" I ask, and she rolls those mossy-green eyes.

My cock twitches. I want to know her more, and I've got plenty of time to do just that now that she's staying here with me for good. I'm grateful to Kai for messing up and spilling the tea about Zion's daughter; it worked in my favor. Now I don't have to give her back. Not now. Not ever. Christmas has come early.

Jingle bells. Batman smells.

"Fuck off," she hisses through her teeth, and I grin.

"Come on, it's well past your bedtime. I'll even sing you a lullaby." As I move closer toward her, she turns, trying to push herself farther against the wall. Like she's afraid of me. My chest tightens.

We don't like that.

Why don't we like that? I'm used to people being afraid of me, but she's different. *Everything* feels different with her.

I reach out my hand to her, but she turns away, staring at the blank wall. Releasing a loud exhale, I grab her arm and pull her up. She doesn't fight me, and I'm glad. I'm fucking tired and I need my sleep.

When we reach the door, I lean around Amirah, my arm sweeping against her pale skin, and a weird sensation moves through me. The hairs on my arms rise, and my breathing picks up. I frown, then shake my head, brushing it off as I twist the knob and push her forward. I have no idea what that feeling was, but it felt good.

We move into the small hallway and then into my bedroom opposite.

I flick the switch on my bedroom wall, my LED lights turning the room blue, and kick the door shut behind me. I release Amirah, and she moves out of my reach, her gaze moving around my room. Graffiti lines every wall.

We write more and more and more when the voices get too loud, about all the things we're going to do. All the people we're going to kill.

My double bed sits in the corner of the room, right up against the wall, and I can't wait to see her between the sheets. I didn't intend to bring her in here to sleep. She should be in my other room, in a cage, like all the other captives I've had in the past. But I don't want her there. At least not tonight. I'm worried she won't be safe. She could try to escape again and might hurt herself. One of the other members of the Hood could hurt her. I don't often have visitors, but if I did, it'd be just like the last time I had something so precious, a jewel so coveted, in my possession.

I can't have that. I want her in here, in my space. I want to watch her. She's different, and we like that. I'm obsessed with her and want to know more.

I turn off the light on my phone but leave the LEDs on, returning the room to its soothing blue. I plug my phone into the charger beside my bed and set it on the small table next to my journal. Amirah doesn't move, stuck at the foot of my bed, her gaze still casting around the room, checking everything out. There's nothing in here apart from my bed, a small table, and a dresser.

I snicker. She's clearly used to big, expensive rooms with walk-in closets and en suites.

"Sorry it's not five stars like you're used to," I say, and Amirah folds her arms over her chest, pushing up her bust. I tear my gaze away, staring at the colorful ceiling.

"You don't know shit about me. Now where am I sleeping?" She huffs, and the corner of my mouth lifts.

Fuck, I love her sass. She isn't what I thought she'd be—full of herself, too good for me and the Hood. Instead, she's curious, smart, and fucking strong.

I point toward my bed, and she wrinkles her nose before moving and sitting down on the edge of the duvet cover.

"I'm not sleeping in here if you are," she says, her voice tinged with worry.

"I'll be on the floor. Hurry up and get inside, so I can read you a story and tuck you in," I say with a playful smile.

Falling back against my pillow, she rolls over so she's facing me and the door.

I move toward my dresser and pull out an old T-shirt that has 18hood written on the front in a graffiti-style script. I throw it to Amirah, and it lands on her body. She doesn't move, her gaze fixed on the door.

"Don't even think about trying to escape again tonight. I'm a light sleeper. And I'm very good at finding little mice who try to run from my clutches."

She releases a heavy exhale, shifting around on the bed, and her black pants cling to her like a second skin.

"Now put that on. Those clothes can't be comfortable to sleep in. Unless you wanna sleep with bloodstains?"

She doesn't move. Whatever.

I kneel down next to my bed, reach into the drawer of my bedside table, and pull out a book full of bedtime stories I've had since I was a kid—the only thing I kept and took with me from home to home.

Amirah rolls off the bed and heads to the adjoining bathroom. When she goes to shut the door behind her, I yell, "Leave it open, and don't you dare try anything. You won't get out of here alive!" I don't trust her enough—what if she grabs something in there and uses it against me as a weapon?

But that would be fun.

I sit back on my bed, clutching the book, trying to keep my eyes downcast to give her privacy. A minute later she emerges, and all the blood rushes to my cock.

My T-shirt rests high above her knees, just covering her underwear. My black heart spurts to life. Fuck me dead. Is she even real? My gaze moves slowly over her milky skin that looks untouched, clean. I want to paint every inch of her in my favorite color: red.

She drops her clothes at the end of my bed and moves over the sheets, brushing past me. I grip the book, and it takes everything in me not to jump on her, pin her down, and claim her. Fuck. No. Stop. I shake my head.

Amirah watches me closely, her brows drawing together. She licks her dry lips and my breathing picks up.

I clear my throat, pushing all my thoughts down into the pits of hell. There's some part of me that doesn't want to scare her away. I want her to see me, really see me.

"I'll read you a bedtime story. Do you know the one about the rich princess who got kidnapped by the sexiest man she'd ever met?" I smile, and she rolls those mossy-green eyes.

She looks around the room, her gaze stopping on my journal, and she points at it. "Read me something from that," she says, not as a question but as a demand.

I snort. "Not happening."

She bats her eyelashes at me, and it feels as though the ground swallows me. Maybe we should? You do use your thoughts for lyrics, so why can't she hear them too?

Fuck, no. That makes you weak.

Does not.

Whatever, pussy-whipped dick.

Shut up. I squeeze my hands around the book.

With a grunt, I reach over, grab the journal, and open it. My words fill every page, and I randomly stop somewhere in the middle. My scribbles stare back at me, words about all the terrible things I've done in my line of work. She doesn't need to know about that. I've never pretended to be a good person, because I'm not.

Everyone is scared of me. I walk into a room and they look away. They move out of my way. No one ever gives me a chance. They think I'm a monster, so that's what I've come to accept, but Amirah is different. She isn't afraid. It feels like she really sees me, and I thought that was what I wanted, but I'm starting to worry it's wrong. She needs to be scared, 'cause I am the devil.

I run my fingers through my hair, then turn the pages until I settle into yesterday's words. When I was feeling trapped. Alone. Torn between two parts of me. That battle I'm constantly facing.

"The walls are closing in around me, suffocating. Taking every last bit of oxygen. I can't breathe; we can't breathe. I open my mouth to scream, but nothing comes out. Will we make it out alive? No, I don't deserve to after what I've done. I'm no saint. I'm the devil. Everyone only sees him. They run. They hide. They scream. I want to make it stop, but the pull is so strong. Who am I without the labels? Nothing. Nobody. I have nothing. Weak. Unhinged. Damaged. That's who we are, who I am. If I was reborn, would I choose differently? Be a better human being? Yes. No. I don't know. I can't stop who I am. The DNA running through my bloodstream—I can't change it. I've done too much. Seen too much. There's no turning back now. My story is set; now I must live with the consequences."

Amirah sniffs, rubbing her red eyes before rolling over, giving me her back, and I close the book, leaving it on my bedside table. I pull back the sheets, and Amirah hops under, covering her body.

"Night, princess," I say, and she ignores me. Did I share too much? Does she hate me now?

She already does. This is your chance to show her that she's nothing. A toy. A pawn.

Her dark-as-night hair lies down her back, and I want to reach out and cut off a strand to keep with me when we're not together.

When we kill her.

CHAPTER THIRTEEN

K^{ai}

I can't fucking sleep. I've been staring at my blank ceiling for hours, wide awake. We need to start moving, taking action, and working out what the fuck we're going to do with her—Amirah—now that she's not going back to the ville. She knows about Cleo, thanks to my big fucking mouth.

Zion was furious, and fuck, I don't blame him. I fucked up. I didn't even realize what I'd done until after. Everything is already difficult with his daughter, and now that Amirah knows, we can't risk giving her back. She could tell The Brotherhood that there's an illegitimate love child living with one of their own, and Zion would never see Cleo again. I won't let that happen. Amirah is staying with us.

I force back the sheets, roll out of bed, and pull on my tracksuit pants, then grab my hoodie on the way out of my bedroom. My trailer is dark and quiet. I flick on the switch in the kitchen and grab my keys off the counter before turning the light back off.

As I head out the front door, the cold night air kisses my bare arms. I pull on my hoodie, leaving the hood up to cover my ears, then walk over to Tate's trailer up the dirt road from mine. I rap my knuckles on the door. It's late, and he's probably in bed. I continue knocking until the lights inside turn on and the door opens. A gun is pointed straight at me, but as soon as he sees me, he lowers it.

"What the hell?" he asks, dropping his gun on the table behind him.

I step back, lighting up a joint. The smoke hits the back of my lungs. Tate meets me outside and runs his fingers through his disheveled dark curls.

"Any updates?" I ask.

He shakes his head. "Still closing in."

I take another deep inhale, kicking off the trailer exterior. "We need to find those guns and fast. Do everything you can," I snap and walk off back toward my place.

I slide into my car and start her up, cranking the heater, then tear out of the trailer park.

We need a long-term plan for Amirah, where she will stay hidden away from prying eyes. Does that mean killing her?

I flinch. I couldn't do that. Not to a woman, even a spoiled princess.

We have control of the Hood, people trust us here, but I don't trust everyone. Given the chance, anyone can, and will, turn their back on you.

Money is a big motivator, and people in the ville have plenty of that. I trust Zion and Bear with my life, but that's it.

My hands grip the steering wheel, guilt weighing heavily on my shoulders. I can't save anyone. Couldn't even save my sister. I've been thinking about her more lately, since Alec—Freya's brother—died. It's bringing back so many memories of that night, and I fucking hate it. It reminds me of how I couldn't save her. How I let her protect me instead of the other way around. I should have protected her. Fuck.

I turn up my stereo, allowing the rap music to drown out my thoughts. Five minutes later, I pull up next to Bear's dirt bike and shut off the car. Stepping out into the cool night, I catch Derek, Spider, and Nick huddled around Derek's car, watching something on his phone. They're supposed to be patrolling, not fucking around. I slam my car door and they look up.

"Fuck," Derek curses, shoving his phone back into his pocket, then stands alert.

I shake my head, moving past the slide and that fucking creepy clown and down the stairs into Bear's den.

The living room is quiet. He's left the lights on, but he isn't here. I move through the curtains and head for his bedroom, through the creepy rooms, keeping my head down until I'm out and in the hallway. Blue light pools through the bottom of Bear's bedroom door, and I open it and step inside.

"We need to—" The words clog in my throat and my jaw drops as my gaze moves from Amirah, who's under the covers on the bed, back to Bear on the floor.

"What the fuck is she doing in here?!" I yell, and Bear jumps up, the blanket falling to his legs, his eyes moving around the room until they land on me. He storms toward me in nothing but his colorful boxer shorts.

"Shh, you'll wake her," he whispers, before forcing me back outside the door and shutting it quietly behind him.

He rubs the sleep from his eyes, and I pace back and forth, anger rolling up from deep inside me.

"Why the fuck is she in your bedroom?" I ask, stopping to stare at him.

He shrugs, then cracks his neck, looking unbothered. He's in way too deep already. This isn't good. I've never seen Bear act like this, and that scares me. I don't know what he's going to do next.

"You never bring people to your bedroom. What's going on?"

Bear bites his bottom lip. "I don't know. It just happened. I was planning on taking her to the other room, then, well, she ended up beneath my sheets. Chill the fuck out. You know how well I take care of my captives," he says, winking with a smug look on his face.

Before I take my next breath, I'm up in his face, my hand around his throat, forcing him back against the wall. He doesn't even flinch, just relaxes into my hold. He enjoys this.

"You didn't touch her, did you?" I ask in a low growl. If he fucking touched her, he's dead.

The corner of Bear's mouth lifts, and I squeeze tighter before releasing slightly. "What if I did finger-fuck her while she was passed out? How does that make you feel?"

I release his throat, landing my fist into the wall right next to his head. Pain rips through my knuckles, and I wish I'd hit that smug look off his face, but I can't. I won't. As much as he pisses me off, he's my best friend. And I know that, deep down, he's one of the good ones—even if he has been fucked up and fucked over one too many times.

"You're fucking sick," I say, and Bear laughs.

"Wow. She's gotten under your skin, too, huh?"

I scoff, taking a step back, but I'm mulling over his words. I have no idea why that got me so worked up, and it's not only the fact that she's distracting him. It's more than that. Something I can't even understand.

"Fuck, no. I just don't want her getting in our way. She's better off in the other room, not here. You'll end up killing her or fucking her, and I don't want that."

Bear looks back at the closed door, then his gaze returns to me. "And which one are you more torn up about?"

I cross my arms over my chest. "Just make sure she's moved by the time I get back here tomorrow," I say before walking off.

Now that Amirah is stuck with us, we need to set some rules. Otherwise, she's going to tear us apart, distract us, and go running back to The Brotherhood. We can't have that. Not when we're so close to finally taking them down. It'll ruin everything.

CHAPTER FOURTEEN

Amirah

As I stare up at the blank ceiling of my new hell, my stomach rumbles, and I can't even remember the last time I ate. Yesterday at dinner? Before Bear kidnapped me. And now, I'm trapped inside a small room, my stomach slowly eating itself.

I've been awake for hours, exploring every inch of this space. The door across from the bed is locked. I've banged on it, screamed, but nobody has come. There are no windows—not even in the tiny bathroom. Nothing I can use as a weapon against my captors.

The walls are closing in around me, and I feel like I can't breathe properly. I miss my room. My clothes. My things. What do they want from me? What are they going to use me for? To have something over The Brotherhood? To use me as a pawn in their war?

The door handle rattles. I sit up straighter on the bed and shuffle up against the wall. Bear walks through the door before kicking it shut behind him. He's carrying a brown paper bag and a book in one hand, clothes in the other.

"Miss me?" he asks, then grins, showing off his perfectly straight teeth.

"You wish," I reply, my stomach rumbling loudly.

A pained look crosses his face, his brows drawing in. He sits down on the edge of the bed, passing me over the bag. He drops some clothes on the bed too. They look worn, old, but there's also some underwear with tags on them. I could cry.

"Got you something to eat from my favorite place and something to wear," he says, and I shake my head. I'm hungry, but what if he poisoned the food? It wouldn't surprise me if he did.

"I'm not eating that," I say, and Bear rolls his eyes.

"Why?"

"Um, because you probably laced it with something."

Bear laughs. "Princess, poison isn't on my weapons list, and trust me, that list is pretty long. But whatever. Starve to death if you want." He shrugs.

Goddamn it. I'm hungry, and I need my energy if I'm going to have a chance of leaving here. I'm no good without the ability to run.

I grab the bag without another thought. I'm about to pass out.

I pull out a large chicken sandwich and fries. My mouth is watering. I take a large bite and groan. So good. I check the wrapper, and it's from Daniel's. Huh? Never heard of that place, which makes sense, considering I've only been over the tracks a dozen or so times. I've certainly never ventured into one of the restaurants.

Bear watches me closely as I demolish every last crumb, a small smile playing on his lips. He shakes his head before opening up his book—the same one he read from last night before I fell asleep and ended up alone in this room.

"Tell me something about you that no one knows," he says, keeping his gaze on the pages of his book.

I push the bag away before leaning back against the wall. I should tell him to fuck off and fight my way out of this room, but I know that's not going to get me anywhere. He'll hunt me down and find pleasure in it.

If I'm going to get out of here alive, I need Bear to trust me. To build a connection between us—and the best way to do that is by giving him a piece of me that's real. That's true.

"I'm not some silly, naïve Brotherhood princess," I say, and Bear chuckles.

"I already knew that. Something else," he says, and I bite my bottom lip. He does?

"There's not much to tell. I guess by being here I'm practically trading one prison for another." Bear frowns. "What about you?" I ask, wanting to change the subject away from me. I've shared enough already, and I'm curious to see if he'll open up to me.

He flips over a couple pages of his book, then looks up, pinning me with his intense green eyes. "Everyone is afraid of me. Hell, even I am sometimes. Nobody understands me. The voices inside my head tell me to do bad things. Terrible things. But when I'm with you, I don't want to listen to them. I fight against them. I don't give in. No one has ever made me feel like this before."

I swallow against the lump forming in my throat. I have no idea what to say back. The more time I'm with Bear, the more I'm seeing him in a different light. He's peculiar—there's no denying that—but it's not all bad. He hides behind his bravado. There's somebody else there inside of him.

He rolls over onto his stomach in front of me, then settles on a page in his book.

"Her screams are all I can hear when I close my eyes. The high-pitched urgency in her voice. 'Help me. Save me. Don't let them hurt me!' But I couldn't help her. The voices taunted me not to be weak, and I wasn't. But I let them win." He lets out a loud exhale. *"I feel like there are two parts of me. Like my soul is split in two. One side, crazy. Dark. Evil. The other, light. Hope. Angelic. Optimistic. I don't let that side out, ever. The dark side always takes control, and it's getting harder and harder to keep him at bay."*

He slams the book shut, and a lone tear falls down his cheek. My heart breaks for him. I want to help, to make it better, but I don't think I can.

He's facing so many demons, and I'm torn between wanting to run as far away from him as I can and comforting him.

CHAPTER FIFTEEN

Amirah

The days have passed painfully slowly. I use an old rusty nail I found under the bed to mark the seventh day here as the sun beams in through the tiny window above the bed. This room is small; a single bed fits in the corner, and there's a tiny bathroom across from it. Nothing else. The white paint is peeling off the walls. It's gross. I prefer Bear's room over this, but I'd never say that out loud.

I drop the nail onto the bed and bring my knees close to my chest. I want to go home, to leave, but I'm locked in here. Trapped.

After that first night, when he read his words to me, I woke up in here. He was gone, and silence consumed me. He visits me every day, telling me stories, sharing his poems, and we've gotten into some kind of routine.

He's only here for a short time, then he leaves again and I'm left alone. I don't like when he's here. I want him to leave, but then when he does, I want him to come back. To have some kind of company. His words are all I can think about. The depth, the emotion in them—it's creating a kind of sick obsession inside me. Every day, I'm craving more.

Being here by myself is driving me crazy. My thoughts won't stop. I need to write them down, but I can't. I don't have a journal. They are bottling up inside of me. The voices won't stop, and it's becoming too much. I need to release them.

I grab the nail and start scraping the end into the dried-up paint next to my bed, writing out how I'm feeling.

Angry.

Broken.

Pissed off.

Prisoner.

Alone.

Useless.

Tears fall effortlessly down my cheeks as the words flow out of me. My shoulders drop, and it's the first time in days that the heaviness inside my chest has released, just a little bit. I've always used my journal to write out my thoughts and feelings. Never did I imagine I'd be scratching them into a wall.

I lean back on my heels, looking at my scribbled words. It's nothing like Bear's artwork in his room. I'd never admit this, but I love what he's done in there. The graffiti of his words covering all the walls—it's a work of art.

Falling back against my pillow, I stare at the blank ceiling. Is my brother looking for me? Freya? Are they going crazy trying to find me? Do they know where I am?

I don't want to just lie here, waiting to be rescued, but there's no escaping Bear's playhouse. The door is always locked and the only window above my bed is padlocked with bars on it. This place is full of surprises and danger.

I have to play this smart. I can't overpower them. They are stronger than me, and even if I could, how would I find my way out? That first night, I tried, but I was trapped before I could even get past the roller coaster.

It makes me think about Jewel and those other girls who still need saving, how they would've felt being trapped. Knowing the enforcer would catch them if they tried to escape. Being so scared, worrying about what's going to happen next. Who will help them if I'm here? Only last week I was ready to save them, to put an end to it.

Now this is my life.

My head is full of thoughts, and it's weighing me down. I feel weak. My body is heavy, keeping me tied to the bed. What's the point in trying? What's the point in anything? I roll over to the side and stare at my thoughts on the wall, reading the words over and over until my eyes become heavy and this madness fades away.

CHAPTER SIXTEEN

Before

Amirah

Clearly, I'm not going to get any help from my brother. But Lily was worried, and now I am too. How can I find Jewel, though? I've done everything. Lily already said she's gone to the police, and they told her she'd probably run away, but we both know it's something more than that.

I get out my phone for the hundredth time to text Freya about this, but I just can't. Not when she's hurting so badly.

Amirah: Miss you, friend. Love you xx

That's what I message instead. At least this way, when she's ready, she knows I'm here for her.

Down the hall, glass smashes. Lucas's laughter drifts to me from a distance.

I smile. There's one person who might be willing to help me—he's certainly not focused on The Brotherhood like Gage is right now. Lucas is distracted. He's angry, confused, and it's perfect for me.

My fists clench at my sides as I rest back against the wall. Fuck Gage and him being too busy to help me, telling me to drop it. I've been fuming since I spoke to him last night. What an asshole. He just wants me to stay hidden and protected behind closed doors, but I'm done with that. I'm trying to help find out where Jewel is. I need to do something, anything, to solve this for Lily.

Cursing travels down the hallway, along with the sound of another glass smashing. I kick off the wall of my bedroom, then move into the hallway. Lucas comes stumbling toward me.

I grab his arms, and he falls into me, laughing.

"What the hell, Amirah?" he grumbles, righting himself. His eyes are bloodshot and the tang of whiskey sours his breath.

"Have you sorted everything out with Freya?" I ask and he scoffs.

"No."

Both of them are hurting after she killed his mom, and it kills me. I'll always have my best friend's back, no matter what, but that doesn't mean I don't feel for Lucas. His heart was broken in the worst possible way. He's like an older brother to me. He's always been around, ever since we were kids.

But maybe his being broken means he'll have more energy for this than Gage did.

"I need your help," I say, looking past him down the hallway. Voices and footsteps get closer, and I grab Lucas's arm, pulling him into the bathroom and closing the door behind us.

"What is it, Amirah? I've got a bottle to finish." Lucas takes a long drink.

I grab my phone out of my pocket, bring up the photo Lily sent me of Jewel, and zoom in on the logo. "Can you tell me if you've seen this logo anywhere before?"

Lucas grabs the phone from my grip and studies it for a painfully long minute. His eyebrows draw inward. "Looks like Bill's Freight," he says.

I open, then close my mouth. I didn't think he'd recognize it so quickly. But he's right. I've only been down to the docks once or twice with Gage, but I remember that logo on one of the containers.

I snatch the phone back off him. I have to go check it out *now*—Jewel could be there.

Lucas grabs my wrist, stopping me. I glare at his bloodshot eyes. He's a mess, and I feel for him, I really do. He just lost his parents. I grew up around them. All they wanted was power, and they'd do anything to make it happen. I never liked Nadine—she was a bitch—but to Lucas, she was love, and this has to hurt. We are both basically orphans.

"Amirah," Lucas says in a deep voice. "You can't just show me this, then leave. What's going on?"

I yank my wrist out of his grip.

Do I tell him about Jewel? It would be easier to find her with his help, but now that I have a lead, and it's pointing to the workers on the docks, I'm nervous to share too much. What if people don't talk to me for fear of him? The Brotherhood controls the docks. But I have to try, and I don't think I can do this alone. Lucas has always protected me, just like my brother. I need his help.

"I have to find out what happened to my friend. She's the one in this photo," I say, and Lucas stares at me for a long second, as if he's connecting the dots between the photo and my mission.

"And you're going down to the docks now, aren't you?" he asks, and I nod. "I'm coming with you." He moves past me before I can say anything, and I follow him quickly down the stairs.

He pushes his feet into his shoes at the front door and stumbles before grabbing the door for support. "They got some stuff down there I want, anyway," Lucas says, and I reach for his pocket. He pushes my arm away.

"You're drunk. You can't drive."

He tosses me his keys, then we head out the front door and into the crisp afternoon air.

I slide into Lucas's bright-red Bentley Mulliner Batur, and Lucas slams the passenger door shut. I hit the start button and shift gears, dirt flicking up around us. I shrug. The gardener can deal with it tomorrow.

I relax back into the leather seat, watching as the world flies past in a blur.

The silence stretches out around us. "What were you planning to do this afternoon?"

"Nothing," Lucas mumbles, staring out the window.

"Sounds eventful. Any news with the Hood?"

"Nope." Lucas brings the bottle to his lips, and I look away.

"Fuck, you're chatty today, aren't you?" I ask as we drive through the city. "Are you okay?"

Lucas snorts. "Wish people would stop asking me that."

"If you need anyone to talk to, you know I'm here for you, don't you?"

Lucas glances my way for the briefest second. There's warmth in his gaze, and the corner of his mouth lifts slightly. "I'm not signing up for your therapy sessions, Amirah, no way in hell. This is me, dealing, and

I'm doing fine," he says, and I sigh. I can't push him; if he wants to talk, he will.

"Offer will always be there for you."

Lucas nods. "I know, lil sis. Now tell me about your friend."

I spend the rest of the fifteen-minute drive to the docks telling him about Jewel, the good times we spent together, and all I know about her disappearance, which is basically nothing. We pull up in the parking lot, the ocean spread out in front of us. I shield my eyes from the bright afternoon sun as I spot large boats sitting docked on the water, with shipping containers nestled on them and more on the docks.

"Let's head to the office first, and I'll ask around," Lucas says. "I have no fucking idea why she'd be here, but I intend to find out. If I discover Bill's Freight is doing anything behind our backs, and especially if they've hurt some friend of yours, then they'll have to answer to me." He hops out of the car and slams the door shut. Thankfully, he sobered up a bit during our trip.

This is the only clue I have from Lily about Jewel, and I don't know if this is going to be a waste of time or if something will come out of it. Still, I'm not going to sit around, doing nothing. Lily needs my help, and I won't let her down. She's been there for me when I needed her, so now I'm returning the favor, and I have to admit . . . I kind of like doing things to make a difference. I've always sat around and watched others take control. But what if I can do this too? What if I can help people in need?

I follow him through the parking lot to the large office building that's surrounded by sheds. Rows and rows of shipping containers line the shore. Workers in reflective vests walk around, talking among themselves. A couple recognize Lucas and pretend to look busy. He ignores them.

Lucas opens the door to the office building and holds it open for me. There's a young guy behind the desk, leaning menacingly over a woman around my age. Her hands are trembling in her lap. What the fuck?

Danger flashes in his eyes, his voice rising. "Do your fucking—"

"Hey!" I yell, and they both look up.

He steps back, and the color drains from his face, but I ignore him, focusing on her. Her cheeks are flushed and her chest rises and falls at a rapid rate.

I cock my head to the side. "Are you okay?"

She quickly nods, but I can see past the façade she's trying to put up.

"Lucas, what brings you here?" the other guy asks, moving around the girl, and she subtly shifts her body away from him.

Lucas pins him with a heavy glare. "Speak to her like that again, and you are gone. Got it, Nick?"

Nick swallows and nods.

"Heard you got a new shipment of supplies that'll heal my broken heart?" Lucas asks.

"Yeah, it's loaded up in the shed, ready for inspection," Nick says, looking up at Lucas like the sun shines out of his ass. Fucking pathetic.

"Oh, what a perfect time for me to show up, then. I'll do some quality control." Lucas grins, his hand on the door. Fantastic. I've come here to get answers about Jewel, and my apparent connection is off to sample some coke.

I cringe. "Lucas, what about—"

"Talk with Chelsea. I'll be back soon." Lucas walks back outside with Nick following closely behind him. What a waste of time. He was supposed to help me, not get sidetracked. Damn him.

Once the door slams shut, the girl behind the desk lets out a sigh.

"What a dick," I say, and she laughs.

"Yeah." She watches me closely. "What are you doing here? You don't act like the usual people who come to pick up shipments."

Straight to the point. I like her already.

"If I show you a photo, can you tell me what container it belongs to or if you recognize someone?" I ask.

She bites her bottom lip, her gaze moving toward the camera, then back to me.

"I'm Amirah Ledger. You won't get in trouble for telling me anything," I say, and her shoulders drop slightly. I reach into my pocket, pull out a fifty from my purse, and leave it hanging between us.

She looks from the money to me before taking it and shoving it inside her top. "I can try, but the containers are all the same."

I pull out my phone, bringing up the photo of Jewel, and pass it over the desk to Chelsea. She takes it and zooms in. Then she frowns, her nose scrunching up.

"I can't identify that container or her, sorry." She passes back my phone and pushes her chair away from the desk. She walks around, brushing past me. "Follow me out," she whispers and opens the front door.

What the hell? I quickly follow her out, down the three steps, and into the parking lot.

We head past one of the sheds, and Chelsea pulls me inside. Half the shed is full of crates that are wrapped in plastic; the other half is empty.

"I can't talk in the office. You never know who's listening, and I don't wanna take my chances," she says, her gaze moving from the roller door and back to me.

"I told you who I am. Anything you say to me won't get you in trouble with The Brotherhood," I reiterate, but she shakes her head.

"It's not your brother I'm worried about. You saw the way Nick treated me." She runs her fingers through her short blonde hair. "I have to be quick. I can't tell you what container that was, but you won't find your friend in a container kept here. They knew you were coming." She stops. Voices grow louder from outside the shed. She leans in, holding on to my shoulder. "They cleared them all out."

My stomach drops.

Chelsea steps back.

"What was in the containers?" I ask, suspecting the answer but wanting to hear it from her.

"You know . . ." She stops as footsteps smack against the concrete floor of the shed. My stomach lurches. I'm going to be sick.

"Here's the second shipment. We're still loading the rest in," Nick says, and Lucas walks beside him. He looks our way, and Chelsea beelines for the door. I quickly follow her until we are a good distance away from Nick and Lucas.

I grab her arm. She looks as white as a ghost.

"If you don't see me again, it's because of this," she says, and I shake my head.

"I won't let that happen."

The corner of her mouth lifts. "They need your help." Then she pulls away from me and hurries back to the office.

I stumble backward until my back hits the shed. This is so much bigger than I thought. This isn't one missing person. If what my gut is telling me is correct, it's more than that—someone is holding a large group of women against their will. Maybe even . . . trafficking them. Does my brother know about this? Is The Brotherhood aware of these shipments?

They have so much on their plates with the new leadership, Lucas's addiction, Freya, and the rumblings of discontent in the Hood . . . I have to do this alone. But I need more power, more resources, and for that, I need The Brotherhood's help. I need my brother's resources.

I want to save them all, but I have to start with saving Jewel.

CHAPTER SEVENTEEN

Z^ion

It's a risk coming to the ville now that we have Amirah. Hell, it always is, but I need to see my daughter. I have to know she's safe. To see her with my own eyes. I can't relax until I do.

The rumble of a car comes down the driveway, and I stay hidden behind the tree until Callan leaves. I check around the quiet street one last time before I move, flicking my hood over my head. My eyes are cast down until I reach the gate, then I open the latch and move toward the backyard.

My heart feels like it's about to explode, and it won't settle until I see her. Voices get louder from in front of me, and I keep moving till I reach the end of the brick house. I peer around and my shoulders drop.

There she is—my little girl sitting on a bright-pink picnic blanket near the pool fence, playing with her doll, mumbling words. The smile on her face brings me to life. She's my world, and everything I do is for her. To make sure she's protected, that nothing can touch her. She's already been through hell, and I want to replace all those memories with love and happiness so she knows nothing bad about this life. She deserves to only see the good. To live in her own little fairy tale.

When I look at Cleo, it's like I'm staring back at Lauren, and it kills me. I still remember the night that changed everything for us—when I lost them both.

I step away from the house, and Cleo's gaze meets mine. Her smile widens, and she drops her doll and runs over to me. Her blonde hair flies with the wind. I kneel down and she falls into my waiting arms. Her little hands clasp around my neck, her strawberry scent calming my racing heart.

She pulls back. "Z, play with me?" she asks, looking up at me with her blue eyes, her hair falling into her eyes. She looks so much like me—her hair, her cheeks, her lips—but her eyes are her mother's, and fucking hell, it kills me that I'll never be able to see her mother again. Does Cleo know that her mom is gone?

I swallow past the lump in my throat. I can't think about that now. I need to be with Cleo.

"Dollies?" she asks, angling her head toward the mat.

I could never tell Cleo no. I'll always give her everything I can just to see her smile. I don't have much, but anything I do have is for her.

I take her hand, and she pulls me back over to the picnic blanket with all her toys. I pick up one of her dolls and start playing along with her. Cleo's four-year-old mind is full of imagination—I love it.

"Who's this pretty lady?" I ask, pointing at the crazy-haired doll in her little hand.

"Molly, and yours is Sky," she says, moving Molly over to Sky. "Can we be friends?" she asks.

I smile. This, being here with her, is everything. "Of course," I say in the girliest voice I can, and soon our two dolls are off to a dance recital together, swirling and twirling in front of the hydrangeas.

Time vanishes as I play with my girl.

The back door slams shut. Natalie, Cleo's babysitter, stands on the back patio and waves me over. I press a kiss against Cleo's head, and she continues playing.

Natalie passes me a soft drink, and I take it.

"Does she know?" I ask, and Natalie sighs, leaning back against the house. I pop the top and take a swig.

"She keeps asking why she won't come back, and I have no idea what to tell her. How do you explain death to a kid? It's all so new. Fresh. It only happened three weeks ago. It breaks my heart," Natalie says, watching Cleo play.

My heart hasn't fully comprehended that the mother of my child is gone. Our relationship ended a long time ago, but I always kept a place for her in my heart. I couldn't give her much, but I could give her a chance at a good life. Daringville was supposed to be safe—the better choice. Now look how that's fucking played out.

"You need to make sure she stays protected at all costs until I can figure out what to do," I say. I can't leave Cleo here forever, not now that Lauren's gone, but I need time to set up a house for her. And I need a plan for someone to care for her, too, while I'm out at work or fighting the war to keep the Hood safe.

"Always, but you have to know that it's getting harder to get you here. Callan has more security. People I don't know hanging around. I can't risk it," Natalie says.

I crunch the can in my hand and throw it to the ground. Fuck. I need to see my daughter. To spend time with her. It gives me a reason to breathe. To know she's okay. Safe.

She's here because I wanted a better life for her, but now that her mother is gone, I'm not sure this is the best place for her. I won't let him raise her by himself. He's never here; he doesn't love her like I do. If he has her, it's going to make it harder for me to see her too.

"I can't not see my daughter," I snap.

Natalie nods. "I know, but I can't exactly risk him finding out. Then you'll never see her again. Hell, I'm just grateful I'm still her babysitter."

"I am too. I have to go, but promise me you'll keep me updated and keep her safe. Please?"

Natalie nods, and I leave after kissing Cleo goodbye, praying that I'll still be able to visit her. From what Lauren told me about Callan, he treated them well. Gave them everything they need, which is more than I could've done. But he didn't raise my girl, Lauren did, and now that she's gone, how can I guarantee Cleo's safety? I'm going to lose my mind worrying about her.

I sneak down the street, looking back over my shoulder and around me. A car drives past, and I hold my breath until it's in the distance. I'm risking my life being here. Someone could recognize me, then it's over.

I'm a block out from the tracks. Hiding behind the trees, I move from one to the other, my throat dry, my heart pounding. I need to get back home. I step out from the safety of the tree line, about to run, then a car with tinted windows flies past and screeches to a halt in front of the tracks, stopping a car coming the other way. Fuck. I jump back behind the tree.

Two guys get out, guns strapped to their thighs. Brotherhood soldiers. One slams his fist down on the hood of the now-still car.

"Get out!" he yells, and the driver of the other car obeys, getting out and placing his hands on the roof of the car. The Brotherhood soldiers move around, opening the trunk.

I inch closer, but not too close.

"Have you seen this girl, Amirah Ledger?" one soldier asks the guy who was driving the car, showing him his phone.

Shit. I've seen her. I wish I fucking hadn't, though.

The guy shakes his head.

"What's your business here?" the soldier asks.

While they are distracted, I move through the tree line until I'm a block away. Then I run as fast as I can back over the tracks, slipping through a gap in the fence when the guards turn their backs. I don't stop until I reach my car a block away.

I slide into my old BMW and warm up the engine before reversing out and onto the street, heading straight for Bear's place.

I hate leaving Cleo. It was easier when her mother was here just three short weeks ago. She gave us time together, but now everything is different. She's gone, and it's getting harder to make arrangements to see Cleo. I won't stop trying, and I won't allow Callan to abandon her. They are searching high and low for Amirah, and it won't be long until they're blowing down our door.

She's been with us a week, and I've spent every moment I can watching her through the cameras. At first, I just wanted to make sure she didn't escape and run back to Daringville and tell them all our secrets, but now it's become more than that.

I want to watch her, to see what she does next. I'm fixated on her, and that confuses the fuck out of me. I never wanted this—to capture someone and hold them against their will. It's not right. But once Kai mentioned Cleo in front of her, all bets were off. I can't risk anyone finding out that Cleo is mine. If they do, death would probably be a better option than whatever punishment they would give my daughter simply for being mine.

I head through the entrance, waving to Derek, who's seated there, and pull to a stop next to Bear's motorcycle. I hop out, bringing my backpack with me. The amusement park is illuminated by the bright, colorful lights beaming through the night. He's always got this place lit up like a fucking Christmas tree.

The gravel crunches under my boots as I move toward the latch door leading me into Bear's living room. The room's dim light comes from the corner, where Bear is sitting in front of the laptop. His shirt is off, his pants are down, and his hand is wrapped around his cock.

"What the fuck?" I growl, but he doesn't even acknowledge me.

He keeps going until he groans and cum rolls between his fingers. Then he cleans himself up with some tissues before tucking himself away and slumping back in the chair.

"Where's Kai?" I ask.

Bear scoffs. "I'm not his mother."

"Well, he sure as shit seems to be treating this place like his home since Amirah came to stay," I mutter. He's practically moved in.

"Now I feel better. Well, it would be better if my cock was inside the princess, but this will do." Bear sighs, still focused on the computer screen, and I roll my eyes, moving closer.

My best friend is a lunatic. It doesn't surprise me that he's obsessed with Amirah Ledger. When something challenges him, it's all he can focus on until he masters it—or breaks it.

Amirah is curled up on the bed, facing the camera, her knees tucked in, and her long, dark hair is matted and greasy, covering half her face. She looks broken and my chest tightens. Where's that fire in her eyes that she had before? It's gone. She's fading away.

"They're looking for her. Saw the patrol on the tracks," I say.

Bear shrugs. "Thought they'd be here sooner. They obviously don't care about her that much."

"Maybe your story about her being at Berkeley was enough to throw them off our scent."

"That, and I heard Spider say they've been going undercover in the diner downtown. Fucking idiots. Like she'd just be hanging out behind the counter."

I shake my head. But for once, maybe Bear's creepy theme park is doing us a favor. No one would ever think we'd keep her in the most well-lit, obvious location in the Hood. I don't even know if Freya understands how much time Bear spends here. We're hiding the princess in plain sight.

I look back at the camera, and Amirah is in the same position. "Did she take a shower today?" I ask and Bear gets up off the chair.

"She still refuses to, but I'm happy to force her in there, if you'd like." The corner of his mouth lifts and his eyes glisten.

I grip the edge of the wooden chair, staring at the screen. She's staring right at me through the camera, like she knows I'm here, watching her. Is someone watching my daughter right now? What would I want for her if she was in this situation?

"No, I'll do it," I say, before moving away.

"Aww, no fun. Maybe we can together?"

"No," I grunt.

"I'll make—" Bear's words follow me out of the room and into the maze of his fun house.

I need to do this for her. To give her something and build a little trust between us. She knows about Cleo and I don't want to risk her safety. I'd go to hell and back for Cleo, and I won't let The Brotherhood princess escape and sacrifice my daughter. I need her to understand the consequences. Cleo is my number one priority; everything I do is to make her life better.

I reach the door to Amirah's room and enter the code on the keypad Kai had one of our friends install. The lock beeps before the door clicks, and I push it open.

Amirah sits up on her bed, her eyes cautious, scanning me up and down. She tucks her hair behind her ear. She's wearing what looks like Bear's black hoodie. It rises, showing off her toned stomach and the top of her lacy underwear. My cock twitches inside my briefs, but I ignore it. She won't distract me.

"What do you want?" Amirah asks, her voice lined with a little bite. She isn't completely broken yet.

"You need to shower," I say, and Amirah shakes her head.

"Yeah, not happening." Amirah bunches up her hair and ties it behind her back.

Her cheeks are starting to hollow out. Her plate on the small table beside her bed looks barely touched. Anger boils up inside me. How long has it been since she's eaten? A day? Has she refused all of our food? Is she worried we've tampered with her meals? What a waste.

"You don't have a choice in the matter. I can either take you kicking and screaming, or would you prefer to go yourself?"

Amirah watches me closely, her eyes turning into slits. That fire is still there.

I step forward, to the end of the bed. She shuffles closer to the wall, creating more distance between us.

"Leave me alone," she growls, and I shake my head.

"Not happening. I'm not leaving until you've taken a shower and eaten the rest of that."

She watches me closely, her gaze heavy. I don't look away. She huffs. "I'm not moving."

I brace my hands on the blanket, close to her legs. "And I'm not playing around."

I grab her thighs and she screams. Her fists slam into my chest.

CHAPTER EIGHTEEN

♔

A mirah

Zion releases my thighs, and I scramble backward on the bed. He points toward the bathroom.

"If you aren't in there in one minute, I'm throwing you over my shoulder and taking you," he says with a deep growl, and I believe him.

I release a loud sigh before pushing off the bed and walking into the adjoining bathroom, my fists bunched at my sides. I'm so sick of these four walls and being held against my will. I want to go home. To be in my own bed and see my best friend. I feel like I'm wasting my life away here, when I could be out there living. Saving lives. Hell, I could be drinking fucking champagne and eating pasta instead of staring at the unenticing food Bear brings in. Nothing like that burger from Daniel's he brought on my second day here. That was yum.

Bracing my hands on the vanity, I stare at my reflection. My hair is a greasy mess, slicked back into a ponytail. My cheeks are hollowing in, and my eyes a darker shade of green than usual. I don't even recognize myself.

I've given up, and that pisses me off. I need to get my strength back, to fight back. I have to play this smart. Smarter than before. I need to gain their trust and then escape once they let their guard down. I tried running before and didn't get far. They were ready, but they won't be when the walls between us lower and they become more relaxed around me. It's clear they're not going to kill me, or they would have done it already. So I'm here for the long haul—which means I stand a chance. I can fight back.

Zion unzips his backpack, pulling out a hairbrush and some little packs of skincare products, placing them on the vanity. "I thought you'd need these," he says, and my heartbeat increases. I've never been so happy to receive beauty products.

Heat presses behind me as Zion reaches around me, his chest brushing against my back. Shivers sprinkle over my arms. Why do I keep getting so turned on by my captors? Is it Stockholm syndrome?

He opens the cabinet and pulls out bottles of shampoo and conditioner, then leaves them on the vanity.

"Get in the shower," he says, his breath hot against my neck. I watch him in the mirror, so close to me. His body feels hot, or maybe it's mine—I don't know. Shit.

"You need to leave," I say, and he shakes his head.

"I want to make sure you actually do it," he says, and my breathing becomes heavier.

"Why do you care so much whether I shower or not?"

"Because, believe it or not, I'm not a monster," he says and I scoff.

"But you're literally holding me against my will," I snap, and a pained look crosses his eyes.

"Not my choice. But if my daughter was in your situation, I'd want her captors to allow her human decencies," he says and I swallow hard. Why does he make that sound so fucking hot? Damn it.

"Where is your daughter?" I ask, and Zion's eyes bore into me like he's seeing right through me. My hands shake and I want to take it back.

When Kai mentioned her and Zion's face fell, I knew I wasn't meant to know about her. Is she in trouble? What happened to her? Why is she over on my side of the tracks? Does anyone else know? Can I help? Is he still with the mother? Oh God. I shouldn't be showering in front of him if that's the case.

"She's not your concern. Just know that I would never allow anything like this to happen to her," he says.

His eyes connect with mine, the dark blue turning a shade lighter. His curly, dirty-blond hair is sitting just above his shoulders. I fight off the urge to reach out and tuck the strands behind his ear. If our situation was different, and I didn't hate him, I'd admit he was hot. Tattoos peek out from the sleeves of his black hoodie but not enough for me to see in detail.

There's this energy around him that draws me in. I want to know more about him, to open him up and see everything he's been through. What damage lies beneath the surface. The darkness in his eyes tells me he's suffered so much in his life already. I crave to find out what, but that's the last of my concerns. I have to remember I'm here against my will. I'm his prisoner.

His arm snakes around my stomach and my legs feel weak. *What is he doing?* He pulls me backward, and I can't fight him. I have no energy left. He turns me around to face him. His fingers move under the hoodie Bear gave me, and my skin burns everywhere he touches. I need to cool down. I need to move away, but I'm rooted to the spot.

My head is screaming at me to run, to push him away, but my body won't move.

He pushes my hoodie up, and I raise my arms without thinking twice. He pulls it off and throws it into the corner of the small bathroom. His gaze doesn't move from mine. He removes my T-shirt, leaving me in my bra and sweatpants. Is he going to take advantage of me? Abuse me without my permission?

Zion's throat bobs and he clears his throat. "You capable of undressing yourself now?" he asks and I open, then close my mouth, unable to form the words. It's as though I'm not even in this room or have any control over myself. I shake my head, and Zion's cheeks turn a shade of pink.

He twirls his finger, and I turn, facing the mirror once again. He moves closer, the warmth of his body hot against my skin. His fingers run down my back, and it's been so long since someone has touched me like this. Gage has scared away all the men I've been with. Goosebumps rise and my legs feel heavy. I grip on to the vanity for support.

I can't look at him, afraid that if I do, I'll do something I regret. It's like I'm watching this unfold from above. I feel faint, all the energy deflated from my body. I can't remember the last time I ate or drank. That's why he's having this effect on me—because I can't think straight. I'm at his mercy. I want to fight back, to tell him to fuck off, but I can't.

His fingers run underneath my bra and he unclips it. The straps slide down my arms, my nipples hardening from the coolness in the air. I peer into the mirror, and fuck, I wish I hadn't. Zion catches my gaze, his blue eyes dark, before he lowers them over my body and I almost break. I'm exposed, and even though I should, I don't want to cover up. The way his eyes take in every curve, there's no judgment. Only lust. Appreciation. Adoration. I feel seen.

His chest rises and falls against my back, his breath hot against my neck. All too soon, it's gone. He steps away, running a hand through his long hair. He points toward the shower, and it takes me a second to get my shit together. When he turns around, I push back from the vanity, letting my bra fall to the ground, then I tug my pants and underwear off.

I turn the shower on and wait a minute before the hot steam fills the air. I don't dare glance behind me, afraid of what I'll see. Still, I do, but I'm confused by the disappointment in his gaze. I don't care what he thinks of me. I should be afraid of what he can do to me, but I'm not.

I step into the warm water, letting it wash away every thought. The pressure isn't strong, not like at home, but it still feels good to get clean.

There's a bang, and I jump, moving back against the shower wall. A door shuts, then Zion's silhouette is there, just outside the glass door of the shower.

He opens the door, passing me some products. He averts his gaze, and I take a deep breath. I need him on my side. There's no question that he feels this attraction between us. I need to use that to my advantage, build some trust between us, if I'm going to make it out of here alive.

"How did you end up with a daughter over on my side of the tracks?" I ask, and I'm met with silence for several long breaths. Shit. Maybe I shouldn't have asked.

"It's a long story," Zion says through the glass between us.

I don't want to push him. I asked, and he doesn't want to answer. Pumping out some of the milk-and-honey body wash onto my palm, I rub it over my arms and legs. The smell reminds me of home. It feels good. A little comforting.

"Would you . . . would you wash my hair?" I ask, pushing open the door. He frowns, his eyes catching mine, and I swallow hard. "I'm too weak to do it myself." It's the truth. I don't have the energy.

He remains silent, and just as I think he's going to leave, he removes his hoodie and T-shirt. A massive tiger sits on his chest with roses and other pieces surrounding it. More ink runs over both his arms, and fuck, he's a work of art. His chest is pure muscle, and I want to run my fingers over each curve. His pants remain on, and I hate that I'm disappointed.

When he clears his throat, my cheeks flame hot. I move back under the water until my body is the same temperature as my face.

"Come here," he says in a deep voice. I step closer until I'm within arm's reach.

He puts some product in his hand before massaging it into my scalp. Slow circles, deep ones, that relax every muscle in not just my head, but my body. I feel . . . treasured. Cared for. There's something deeply intimate about the act. My muscles relax, and for one moment, one brief moment, it's like I'm somewhere else, someone else.

"Lauren, Cleo's mother, and I were together since we were seventeen. She was the first person I loved," Zion says, and I don't utter a word.

He nudges my shoulder, and I step back under the water. Running my fingers through my hair, I wash out the shampoo.

"She got pregnant at twenty-one. We didn't plan it, but it changed everything for us. She was working at a club when we found out."

I look at him over my shoulder. His hands start to shake at his sides, and there's a faraway expression in his gaze.

What club? I want to ask, but I can't interrupt him. This is his story, and I'm guessing it's not easy for him to tell.

"She wanted to keep the baby, but we were living in a trailer. There were fights all the time, and the drugs . . . my mom was into it bad. I didn't want my kid growing up like that. One of the guys at the club, I knew he was into Lauren. So I told her to try to seduce him. Let him believe the kid was his. That way, they could have a better life."

"You gave up the woman you loved . . . to save her life?" I ask, holding back the tears.

"I gave up two women I loved." Zion sniffs. "Lauren let me sneak over the tracks to see Cleo a lot—like every week or so. Cleo thinks I'm her mom's brother. I think Lauren convinced Callan I was an imaginary friend." His eyes glisten over, and I want to take all the pain away.

I pull him into the shower. He kicks one of the bottles of shampoo, and it rolls along the floor. My arms wrap around his waist. My head is resting on his chest. His heart is ringing in my ear. He stiffens before melting into my body, his jeans now soaking wet.

"She died in the explosion," Zion whispers, and I freeze.

I can't breathe. Everything closes in around me. I rip myself out of his embrace, stumbling back until my back hits the tiles.

He looks at me and my whole world crumbles. Tears run down his face, blending in with the stream of the shower.

"I'm so sorry," I say, like that will help, but I know better. Words won't heal this. The wounds must still be so fresh. They haven't been together for years, but she's still the mother of his kid.

We stay like this for seconds, minutes, staring at each other. Time vanishes. Disappears around us.

"It's not your fault," Zion says and steps closer. He leans down, grabbing the conditioner. As he pours product into his hand, I turn around, and he brushes his fingers through my hair.

Then he massages my scalp in slow, dizzying circles I feel every-where. I should be comforting him, not the other way around. My eyes flutter shut. Fuck, this is good. I don't think I've ever had someone wash my hair for me—well, apart from my hairstylist, but it's never felt this good before. Never this . . . sensual. My knees become weak, and I need to hold on to something before I fall to the ground.

I reach out, bracing my hand on the shower screen. I'm trying to hold it for support, but it's slippery and wet. What would it be like if I turned and kissed him? What would happen then? Fuck. This is wrong, but it feels so right. I should be fighting him, using this moment of weakness against him, but it's impossible when it feels this good. I moan and Zion stops.

Damn it. No, that did not just happen.

All too soon, his fingers are gone, and I let out a loud exhale before stepping back under the warmth of the water and letting the waterfall consume me. I don't dare open my eyes. I can't look at him. Whatever just happened wasn't supposed to. I got caught up in the moment. The ache between my legs is evidence of that.

When the loud bang of the bathroom door echoes around me, I open my eyes. He's gone, and I'm left wanting more, forgetting that maybe, while he was distracted, I could have run. I could have escaped.

CHAPTER NINETEEN

B ear

The door to my living room opens and slams against the wall, followed by the swish of the curtain. I sit up straighter on the couch, my notebook falling beside me. Zion storms through the room without so much as a glance my way before he leaves up the stairs, taking a wave of angry energy with him. Probably back to his trailer.

The corner of my mouth lifts, and I flip the pen around my fingers. What did our little princess do now? I knew she'd be fun when I first laid eyes on her. I was itching for a challenge, something that would light that fire inside me, and she's exactly what the doctor ordered.

Judging by Zion's swift exit, she's not just affecting me but him, too, and that's fucking perfect. Zion needs something to loosen him up a little. He thinks I don't notice how cut up he's been ever since his bitch of an ex died, and he's been trying to see his kid, but I do. A distraction will be good for him.

I grab my notebook and pen, move toward the desk, and sit down on the chair to watch the live camera feed. Steam comes from the closed bathroom door. What's she doing in there? What happened with Zion? I need to know. I need to see her.

Opening up my journal, I start scribbling down lyrics.

She's an obsession, my only desire.

If we can't have her, no one can.

What's inside that mind of hers? Can we split her skull and find out?

I'm never letting her go. Oh, fuck no. She's ours. Forever mine.

Movement catches my gaze on the screen, and I lean forward. Amirah emerges from the bathroom, a towel covering her chest. Her long, wet hair dangles down her back. I want to wrap every strand around my fingers and pull, watching the pain on her features. My cock stirs.

She moves toward the bed, dropping the towel. My heart skyrockets. Holy fucking Christmas. Jackpot. Jingle bells. I grip the laptop screen, trying to bring it closer. Her curves, her ass. I need to lock her up in a display cabinet in my bedroom.

She bends over, her pussy teasing me. I reach into my pants, my cock in my palm, and it's only been an hour since I last jerked off to her, but hey, I'm ready to go again. She's such a fucking dirty little cunt, my captive. She hops under the blankets, and I curse. No. I want to see her. She leans back against her pillow, staring up at the ceiling.

The sheets start to move, and my eyes widen. This just got even more interesting. Did Zion turn her on? Is she . . . is she flicking the bean? Damn it. I wish I watched what happened before this.

Her eyes flutter shut, and her mouth opens just a fraction. She's touching herself. Fuck me sideways. I need to get in there. My cock feels heavy in my palm. It needs to be inside her. I imagine her warm cunt tightening around me.

The sheets move up and down. I follow her pace. She says something, but I can't fucking hear her. Where's the fucking volume on this fucking camera?

We need to give her a helping hand. Now. Go.

I push back, the chair falling onto the ground with a bang. I grab the new journal I brought for her before shoving my cock back into my pants, and I move like my ass is on fire. I need to hear her come apart. Within seconds, I'm outside her door. I press my ear against it. Her heavy breathing sends me over the edge. She's so close.

She moans, and I put the code in and rip the door open. She screams as I storm over and rip the blankets off. Her finger rests between her inflamed folds. Her large tits beg me to suck them.

"Want me to finish you off?" I ask, grinning.

A wild look crosses her eyes. She shakes her head, but all I can see is approval in her gaze. I throw her journal onto the bed before crawling closer to her, and she doesn't move or push me away. I sit over her legs, then grab her hand, bring her fingers to my nose, and inhale. Her sweet, tangy scent fills every part of me. Fucking hell.

Her chest rises and falls to the beat of mine. Her silver necklace with the initials AL sits perfectly above her breasts. I need it as a souvenir. I grab the chain and pull. It snaps and falls from her neck, and she gasps. I shove the necklace into my pocket, wanting something of hers to keep.

"Give it back!" she snaps.

"It's mine now."

Her eyes darken and her lip curls back in a snarl.

She's taunting me. Daring me to go further. I bring her fingers into my mouth, licking each digit clean. Her mouth opens, like she wants to say something, but she doesn't.

I'm the devil and she's my prize.

The door opens. Amirah looks toward the intruder, her eyes widening, but I don't move a muscle.

"Get the fuck off her, Bear," Kai says in a deep voice, and I laugh, pulling her fingers out of my mouth. She retracts her hand from my grip.

"Nah, she's having fun," I say, and Amirah shakes her head.

"Like fuck I am. Get off me, you psycho." Amirah's words feel like a bucket of ice-cold water thrown over my head.

I frown, looking at her. Psycho. I hate that word. Anyone who has ever called me that ended up dead. I can never hurt her, but that doesn't mean I won't punish her. People don't understand me, us, but I thought she did. I thought she got my weirdness, but apparently not. I roll off her and storm away. Kai says my name, but I ignore him, my shoulder banging into him on the way out.

I need to do something, anything, to release this anger. Confusion. Sadness. They're all rolling around inside me. She called me a psycho? Not my princess. It feels as though she stabbed me in my cold, broken heart. And I didn't even get to finish her off. Fuck my life.

***

I've been sitting back against the door to her room for hours. Replaying what she said. Psycho.

Just kill her. Make her pay.

I grip a handful of my hair, pulling. Pain rips through my skull. Why does it hurt so much? Why did she say that to me? I thought she liked me.

Who cares? She's the enemy.

Footsteps come from the corridor. Zion walks toward me, holding a plate of food for Amirah. I stand, taking it from him.

"I'll bring it in," I snap, and Zion opens his mouth, but I glare at him. I'm not in the mood to deal with him.

He raises his hands, taking a step backward. "Whatever," he mutters, before walking away.

I open the door, and Amirah looks up from the bed. I bring the plate of spaghetti over to her, and she takes it from me and places it on the bed. "Thanks," she says.

I sit on the edge of the bed. Silence drags out between us.

"Why did you call me that?" I ask.

She finishes off a bite. "What?"

"Psycho?"

Amirah's eyebrows fall, and she cocks her head to the side. Her gaze is heavy on mine, and I swallow hard. Maybe I should go. This is silly. Stupid.

Punish her. She deserves it.

"Oh, I didn't realize . . . I hurt your feelings?" she asks, reaching out to place her hand on my thigh, and I nod, casting my gaze down.

So weak.

Shut up. I place both of my hands over my ears in an attempt to block out the noise inside my head, squeezing my eyes shut. The bed dips, and hands cover mine.

"Look at me," Amirah says, and I obey, staring into her mossy-green eyes. "I'm sorry. I didn't mean to upset you like this," she says, and my heart skips a beat.

"Do you think I'm a psycho?" I ask, my voice trembling, and she shakes her head.

"I think the world doesn't understand you . . . but I am starting to," she says.

She drops her hands from mine, and I smile.

She really sees me. Understands me. God damn, I'll remember this moment forever.

CHAPTER TWENTY

K ai

Images of her naked curves, her bare pussy, cling to every cell of my mind. It's all I've thought about for the past two days, and fuck, I don't know how I feel about that. The cold water runs over me in an attempt to cleanse me of my sins. The pressure of my shower is shit, but it's better than nothing.

My hand finds my hard cock, and no matter how many times I've given in and jerked off, it's not enough.

I hate myself for feeling anything toward Amirah fucking Ledger. She's the enemy. But the longer we have her, the more I'm considering handing her back over. She's distracting us all. I can see it in Bear—he's obsessed and won't do anything but stare at her. I haven't seen Zion in days, and we're supposed to be preparing for war.

I tug my cock in frustration, just imagining every single curve of her body, the way Bear tasted her . . . I want to know exactly how she tastes. I brace my hand on the vinyl tiles just as there's a knock on the bathroom door.

"Fuck off," I growl, and the door opens.

Bear leans back against the doorframe, his gaze running from my cock back up to my eyes. "Oh, don't tell me she's getting to you too? Want me to lend you a hand?" He smirks.

I ignore him, closing my eyes. I need this release, and I won't let Bear ruin it for me. Images of Amirah's curves, her mossy-green eyes, fill my mind. I imagine my name spilling from her lips. Fuck.

"Oh yeah, brother. Imagine me licking her wet cunt. Every last drop of her sweet, tangy juices. They fall down my chin, and it's the best fucking meal I've had in weeks." Bear laughs.

"Fuck!" I groan and shoot my load, my cum hitting the shower wall. I step back into the cold water, drowning out Bear.

"We've gotta do something about her," I say, shaking water out of my hair.

"Probably, but she's my captive, and what I say goes." Bear's voice is low and deep. He's so fucking obsessed with her.

"My fucking point exactly. She's distracting us all from taking over the ville," I say.

Switching off the shower, I step out, and Bear hands me a towel.

"Yeah, we can't do anything about that," he says, checking his phone before looking back up. "Oh, that loser Tate came around looking for you, so I drove him right out of my theme park to here." Bear yawns.

All I want to do is lock myself in my trailer and spit out the words, the feelings lodged in my chest. I want to find the rhyme, the rhythm in this madness that we call life, but that's not going to happen. With Amirah as our captive, and now Tate saying there's a problem, it never ends. Will there ever be a time when we can just live and not be in survival mode? Fuck, I hope so.

"Tell him to meet me outside," I say, and Bear walks back out the bathroom door.

This past week, I've spent more time at Bear's than at my own place. I don't want to admit to myself that the reason is anything other than practical. Bear needs the extra security. If Amirah escaped and went back to them with the information she has, I would never forgive myself. I'm the reason she knows about Cleo, and I won't ruin Zion's chances of bringing her home. He wanted to have everything ready for her. The home, money, security.

I dry myself off and put on some gray sweatpants and a black T-shirt with 18hood written on the front in white.

After grabbing my phone from beside my bed, I shove it into my pocket and head out of my room. Down the corridor, putting one foot in front of the other until I'm outside. The dark, cloudy sky greets me, thunder rumbles, and it perfectly resembles how I'm feeling.

Tate is leaning back against his car in the middle of the theme park. He pushes off and meets me. He moves from one foot to the other, staring over my shoulder at the ridiculous roller coaster behind me that looks like it's about to fall apart.

"Have you got guns? Do you know where they are?" I ask, desperate to know if he has the missing piece we need to invade Daringville—weapons.

"We're so close. I heard from Jack there's a lot of armed guards around the town hall," Tate says, and I frown. "That doesn't make sense. Why guard a blown-up building?"

"My thoughts exactly. They must be there," Tate says.

"Fuck! How the hell can we get the weapons from right in the center of town?" This isn't good.

"I got nothing, but right now, we've got bigger problems," Tate says.

"What is it?" I ask, and he meets my gaze. "Security breach at the tracks. Brotherhood are there, demanding a meeting with you."

Fuck. Do they know we have Amirah? Are they wanting to trade with us? I can't let that happen yet, not while Zion's daughter is at stake. I won't let anything happen to her.

"Gather up the gang and meet us there," I say, and Tate nods, sliding back into his car.

I pull out my phone, hitting call on Zion's name.

"Yeah?" he answers.

"Get down to Bear's. We've got a meeting request."

Zion grunts and hangs up.

The door behind me slams shut, and Bear comes out, sliding on a hoodie. "What'd he want?" he asks, and I grab a rolled-up blunt from my pocket and light it up. The smoke fills my lungs and calms the rapid beating of my heart just a bit.

"Brotherhood at the tracks. They wanna meet," I say, taking another drag.

Bear's mouth curves, and he cracks his knuckles. "Perfect timing. I'm feeling like shedding some blood today," he says, and I shake my head.

"What about her?" I ask.

Bear lifts out his phone, typing away. "Got her on surveillance, and Derek is staying back in case she tries anything, but the door to her room's locked, and so is the front entrance. There's no way she's getting out of there," he says, and I nod.

He reaches out, and I pass him the blunt.

A couple minutes later, Zion pulls up on his motorcycle and hops off, placing his helmet on the seat. "Who we meeting?" he asks, taking the blunt out of Bear's fingers and bringing it to his lips.

"Brotherhood wanna talk at the tracks," I say.

Zion's throat bobs. "Do they know about Amirah?" he asks, staring over my head at the park.

"I don't think so, but we need to be ready for anything. Tate's gathering some backup and meeting us there. Let's go," I say, moving toward my car.

I drop into the driver's seat. Gage either knows or suspects something, and it could go one of two ways—no one leaves the tracks alive, or it'll be the kickoff for this war. We aren't ready yet. We need more weapons, more power to overthrow them. Whatever happens on these tracks is going to force us into action.

"You know this is the perfect opportunity to kill off the precious leaders of The Brotherhood. Cut the heads straight off the snake," Bear says from the back seat, meeting my gaze in the mirror. The corner of his mouth lifts in a smirk.

He's right, but we can't. It's too risky.

"We need our weapons that Dominic promised us. We don't have enough power to kick off the war yet," I say, and Bear rolls his eyes, falling back into his seat.

"And we need my daughter safe," Zion says. "I'm so close to having enough rent to get a house for her, something better than my piece-of-shit trailer. Give me a little more time to get her out, then you can do whatever you want."

"How much time *exactly* do you need?" I press.

"Give me a week," Zion says. "Maybe someone at work has a place they're renting out. And I need to find a fucking nanny I can trust over here."

"She could always stay here," Bear offers with a creepy smile.

Zion shudders. "This is no place for a little girl."

I agree.

It's time to stop playing small. We need to make moves. Big moves. And now that we have The Brotherhood princess, we can use her to our advantage.

I switch gears, flying out of Bear's theme park onto the dirt road and heading straight for the meeting point. Fuck, I hope Freya stayed home and isn't with them. They need to lock her up so she's safe and protected, but they won't. She's too smart for them; she'd break out in seconds. I miss my best friend, but I'm done trying to convince her to return home. She's made her bed, and she's sleeping with our enemy. I'll always love her, but I have to let her go. Focus on protecting the people who are on our side, who look up to me, to us, as their leaders.

The tracks come into view, and there she is, her long brown hair up in a high ponytail, her arms crossed over her chest, and a look of fire in her eyes. I smile. Thank fuck Freya hasn't lost that yet. Gage, Lucas, and Hazen are with her, looking pissed off.

Tate is on our side of the tracks with about twenty men scattered around the road and outhouse. They aren't carrying guns, but The Brotherhood doesn't know that. Lightning pierces the sky. A storm's rolling in.

I pull up, and as Bear opens his door, I reach out, grabbing his arm. He glares at my fingers around his forearm, but I don't let go.

"Don't do anything unless I say. Got it? I wanna see how this plays out first," I warn, and Bear rips out of my grip, slamming the door behind him and completely ignoring my warning. Fucking hell.

Let the games begin.

CHAPTER TWENTY-ONE

B efore

Amirah

I slam my bedroom door shut as hard as I can. It rattles, and I want to scream. I spoke with Gage when we got back from the docks, and he gave me literally none of his time. Jewel has been moved from the docks. I've googled Bill's Freight, and nothing interesting comes up, so I'm at a dead end. That was my only lead, and I've blown it.

Then there was a huge explosion at town hall that took so many lives and left Freya in the hospital! I have to get this all out. I need a release.

I race over to my bed and pull out my journal from under my pillow. After grabbing the pen from its holder, I start writing. Words fly onto the paper. I can't keep up. My hand shakes, but I push down on the pen harder, letting it all out.

Men are so predictable, and Gage is such an asshole. I went to him for help, to have more power within The Brotherhood so I could dig deeper into Jewel's disappearance and those shipping containers.

What did my brother say to that? I'll tell you. He told me to go paint my fucking nails. What a dickhead. I tried to tell him about Jewel and the shipping containers, but he shut me down. I thought he could help, but he didn't even give me the time of day. If you want something done right, you need a woman.

I'm still nervous to do this alone. It's so much bigger than I thought. Maybe I should ask Freya about it. She might be able to help, but I still feel like I can't burden her with this. Especially after the explosion and hurting herself. She's got too much happening. I have to do this by myself.

I close my journal and place it back under my pillow. A small weight lifts off my shoulders. I pull out my phone and hit call on Lily's name. She answers in two rings.

"Hey, darling girl, any news?"

"Hey, Lily. You busy?"

"Just about to leave for work. Everything okay? Any updates? Did anyone get hurt in the explosion?"

I sit up straighter, holding the phone to my ear. "No, we are all okay, thank goodness. Nothing yet with Jewel, but I had a lead that took me to the docks. Did Jewel ever say anything about visiting there?"

The line stays silent for a couple of long seconds. "No, not to me. What would she be doing in that place?" Lily asks.

"I'm not sure yet, but I'm working on it. I'll keep you updated, okay?"

She sniffs, and my heart breaks for her. I can't imagine what she's going through, not knowing where her daughter is.

"Okay, darling girl. Thank you for the update. I love you," she says, and I drop my head into my other hand.

"I love you too."

I hang up, then fall back against the duvet, staring up at the white ceiling. This situation both terrifies me and gives me a purpose—to save them all and solve this mystery.

My phone vibrates next to my head, and I open it to find a text from Freya's mom.

Freya is out of the hospital

These other women need saving, but first, I need to make sure my best friend is okay.

CHAPTER Twenty-Two

Bear

I laugh to myself. Kai has lost his goddamn mind if he thinks I'll listen to his orders. I play by my own rules—always have and always will. I don't get told what to do. Hell, even I can't control the actions that I take half the time. There are multiple voices inside my head, and I never know which one is coming out to play.

Moving around the car, I stalk closer to the tracks, stopping on our side. I wink at Freya, and she smiles. Though I miss her, she'll never be one of us again. I've accepted that, unlike Kai. She'll always have a place in his heart. That makes him weak. The fact that he has a heart. It'll get him killed.

Gage stands next to Freya with his shoulders pushed back, a fierce look in his gaze. He appears to be ready to fight and, fuck, that makes me giddy. As I bounce from one foot to the other, my eyes clash with Lucas, and I wave at him. He flips me off, and I snort.

"Hello, my little pup," I say, and Lucas steps forward. I meet him in the middle of the tracks, his chest touching mine.

"Fuck you," he seethes and shoves me.

I stumble back a step, and my chest heaves. I lick my lips, ready to cause mayhem.

Kill him.

A hand lands on my chest, holding me in place, and Hazen pulls Lucas back.

"Enough!" Gage booms, and I shove my hand into my pocket. My fingers wrap around Amirah's necklace that I ripped from her neck. A sense of calmness washes through me; it feels nice.

Not as nice as blood would, running down your hands. Kill Lucas.

Fuck. I miss her. I wanna go back. What if she's escaped? She can't. We haven't played with her enough yet. She's like a puzzle to me. So many pieces. So much to discover and put together. I want to know everything.

"What do you want?" Kai asks, sliding up next to me.

I keep holding on to Amirah's necklace. It's grounding me, keeping me here.

"Not sure if you've heard, but my sister, Amirah, is missing," Gage says, and I smirk.

Freya watches me closely, her head cocking to the side. She's trying to read me, but she won't get anything. I won't say or do anything. I don't want Amirah going back to them. She's ours now. They'll have to kill me before I let her go.

"Yeah, we heard, but that doesn't explain this," Kai says, pointing between us.

"Do you have her?" Freya asks, stepping forward in front of Kai.

I see what game she's playing—using Kai's weakness for her against him.

"No," he says, and his response is met with silence. Freya watches him closely, no doubt checking for anything that'll give him away, but he remains stoic.

"And we're supposed to believe you?" Gage huffs. "We're coming over to check."

"No, fuck off. You take one step over these tracks, and the war has begun," Kai growls.

"Last we heard, she was in Berkeley at some college there," Zion says.

Gage's fists ball at his sides. He's on edge. I should feel sorry for him—he's lost his precious little sister—but I don't, because she's mine now, and I'll never let him have her again.

He took advantage of her. She's not some stupid Brotherhood princess who should be locked up in a castle. No, she's so much more, and I'm not done playing with her. Not finished digging deep into her psyche to peel back the layers until I find the real her.

"We already checked there. We tore that place apart, and unless she's buried—and surely no one would be that stupid—she ain't there. So you're lying to us," Gage says.

"The fuck you say?" I roar and race toward him. I grab him by the shirt, pulling him to the ground as I punch his face. "You don't call me a liar!" But what I really mean is, you don't joke that Amirah could be dead. How dare he?

I punch him, and he punches back. Blood flies. Chaos erupts around us, and I couldn't be happier.

We roll around on the ground, Gage on top of me, then me on top of him. Fists fly everywhere. Pain burns into my flesh, just the way I love it. I flip Gage over, pinning him down on the ground, my knees holding him as he thrashes around.

"Aww, Gage, remind me: you like having a dick up your ass?" I ask, and the look of horror in his gaze tells me exactly what I wanted to hear.

He spits, and it lands on my cheek. I smirk, letting the wetness slide from my chin and onto his T-shirt.

"Get the fuck off me!" he yells, and I lean forward, my cheek resting against his, my breath against his ear. He moves, kicking, trying to get free, but I'm stronger than he is. My hold is too powerful for him.

"But I wanna play with you," I whine in my best little kid voice. I laugh, joy bubbling up inside of me. Sure, Gage is stronger than Lucas. He throws a harder punch, but I could still beat him. Mess with him until he's begging me to stop.

Gage rams his fist into my stomach. I sit back ignoring the pain, looking around. Kai is in a fistfight with Hazen. Lucas has Zion in a headlock.

A gunshot rings through the air, and everyone freezes. Hazen moves his pistol, aiming it at Zion's head. I see red and jump up, smashing my fist into Gage's face before I let him go and stalk toward them. Zion shakes his head at me, but I don't stop until I'm pulled backward by Kai, who holds on to me. Fuck.

"Enough! This isn't what I came here for. I want my sister. You have forty-eight hours to bring her home or find her. This place is the only one we haven't searched. If she isn't back before then, I'm ripping your whole town apart, and you'll pay with your lives," Gage says, shoving Zion away. He stumbles over to our side of the tracks.

I pull against Kai's restraints. *We want blood. More blood.* My gaze moves from Gage to Lucas. He wipes away blood pouring from his nose, and my heart warms. That's something. A little taste.

I wave at him, and he flips me off before walking away. Kai doesn't release his hold until the others are in their cars. I stumble forward, my hands trembling. Kai follows me.

"What do we do now?" Zion asks, running his fingers through his hair.

"We either hand her back over, or we prepare for war," Kai says.

Zion shakes his head. "No, she knows about Cleo. We can't do anything until I have my kid back with us. Until I know she's safe."

"What about the home you wanted for her? The nanny?" Kai asks, frowning.

"I'll have to make do with what I got." Zion shrugs. "She won't be safe if we go to war. I need her here with me now."

"We'll make a plan, brother." Kai claps him on the shoulder.

"Only way Amirah is leaving now is in a body bag," Zion says, his voice dropping.

Anger builds inside me. I won't ever let that happen to her. She's mine now. Ours. Only I can hurt her, but I'd never kill her.

The ride back to my place is silent. Kai drops me off, then leaves. Good. I just want to be with her. Without anyone else. Just us two. What's she been doing? I hope she's missed me.

I reach for Amirah's necklace in my pocket, wanting that familiar calming sensation to bring me some peace before I walk in, and my stomach drops. Fuck.

It's gone.

CHAPTER TWENTY-THREE

A mirah

I'm going insane, staring at the white ceiling of this room that's been my prison for ten days. I need to get out. Fresh air. I've been running laps around the room just to burn off energy. The food they've been bringing me is boring, bland, but it's better than starving to death.

Bear came into my room last night. I felt his presence, but I didn't make a sound or move. He slipped inside the sheets and pulled me against his body. His warmth wrapped around me, and I fell back asleep. I woke to an empty bed and an even more confused heart. Why do I find comfort in him when he's the one who took me? What makes him feel so . . . safe?

I haven't seen Kai or Zion since yesterday. It's quiet inside Bear's playhouse. Maybe they've left and deserted me for good? Doubt that.

I should be trying to escape, but it's useless. I've looked everywhere inside these four walls, and there's no getting out of here unless someone lets me out or leaves the door open. Bear may be a lot of things, but he isn't stupid. I'm his captive, and he won't let me go without a fight.

The way he looked at me when he grabbed my fingers covered in my own juices and put them in his mouth . . . fuck. Warmth pulses through my body just thinking about it, and that worries the hell out of me. He captured me, took me against my will, and I'm his prisoner. He shouldn't have this effect on me. I hate him. Even as I think those words, I hardly believe them anymore.

Being here, being around him, has become familiar.

Now I'm sounding like the crazy one. But Bear doesn't scare me. I think, deep down, he just wants to be accepted, even loved, and I don't believe he's ever felt that way before. He left a new journal on my bed the other night, and it's been my savior.

The more time I spend with each of them, the more confused I get. I may still be a prisoner, held against my will, but I feel like I'm important when I'm around them. I feel seen.

The door creaks open, and I sit up straighter on my bed. Kai comes in carrying tray of food, and my stomach rumbles.

He places the tray down on the bed, his biceps bulging. My fingers grip the duvet as I hold back the urge to reach out.

"Have you showered today?" he asks, his voice deep.

I nod, reaching for half of the toasted sandwich. I expect him to leave, but he doesn't. He sits there silently while I eat. All I can hear is the beat of my heart and the crunch of bread.

In some fucked-up way, being around Kai makes me feel protected. Safe. He would never hurt me. Like he always protects Freya. I once thought he really loved her, but I've come to see it's more brotherly love than the romantic kind. Is there someone else he has feelings for? He's not wearing a ring, but does he have a girlfriend? A sidepiece? A whole harem of women?

We've spoken a little each day when he's come to bring me food and take my laundry. But never anything deep—never anything beyond surface level.

"Do you have family here?" I ask, and a muscle in his neck ticks.

He looks around the room before settling his intense brown eyes back on me. There's a lost look in them, and I think I've just hit a nerve.

We sit in silence, both eating. I finish my sandwich, and when I think he won't answer, he opens his mouth. "I had a sister when I was a kid," he says quietly, and I rest back on my hands. *Did*, past tense.

"What happened to her?"

He lets out a heavy exhale, then shifts on the bed to face me, and I can't look away. "She died." His voice falls and tears pool in his eyes. Poor guy.

I rest my hand on his, and he doesn't pull away. "I'm so, so sorry," I say, biting my lip. "How?" I ask, and part of me isn't sure I want to know.

"Your precious Brotherhood killed her." His eyes turn into slits, and he pulls his hand from under mine. It feels like a bucket of cold water has been thrown over me.

"Oh my God," I say. "They wouldn't." My chest rises and falls fast. There's no way my brother or Lucas or Hazen did this. They'd never hurt a woman. No.

Kai pushes off the bed and stands in front of me. "They did. Right in front of me." His eyes are watery, and I want to comfort him.

But when I reach out, he steps backward. My heart aches for him, even as anger rolls beneath my skin. I can't believe this.

"Tell me who," I say before I can think.

Part of me wants to know—the other doesn't. I grew up inside The Brotherhood. They are my family. Even though they aren't good people, they'd never harm a kid. I refuse to believe it. But the look on Kai's face, the anger radiating from him—it's not fake, and that kills me.

"We lived in one of those Brotherhood-controlled units. You know the type—not enough space to swing a cat, no air conditioning, but it was a roof, and it kept us safe after my parents died. But then came the eviction notice plastered on our door." He lowers his gaze to the ground, and I want to reach out to comfort him. To take away the pain.

"We ignored it because we had nowhere else to go. It was either a roof over our head or the streets. We didn't have a choice." Kai runs a hand through his mousy-brown hair.

There's pain still evident in his gaze. He lives with this every day. I wish we could burn all the rules to the ground. That there wasn't a divide between us. Between classes. Rich versus poor. Being here, inside this amusement park, I've only seen a little glimpse of what life is like in Daringhood. It's so different from what I'm used to. At home, I have someone looking after me. Picking up everything. I literally don't have to do a thing. Here, they have to work for what they need. Without it, there's no food. No resources. No clothes. I can't even imagine what it's like on the streets.

"Part of me wishes that we had listened to their warnings. That we'd left before it was too late. But I can't change what happened next, as much as it kills me." Kai bites his bottom lip, and I inch forward on the bed.

I stay silent, giving him the space to talk. To tell his story.

"They came in the middle of the night. Ripped down our door. I still hear her screams." He stops, his forehead scrunched together.

"She protected me, pushed me into the closet and shut me inside. She always did everything in her power to hide me from the bad in the world. I didn't want her to leave me alone." His voice drops, and my heart breaks for him. For her.

"How old were you?" I ask.

Kai's throat bobs. "Seven." Just a kid.

"I peered through the crack in the closet. My sister stood in the bedroom, and then *they* came in." Kai's chest rises and falls.

"Who?" I lick my dry lips, my grip tightening around the duvet.

"Hazen, Lucas, Gage, and Dominic," he says, and the ground beneath me swallows me whole.

No. I don't prompt him to continue. I'm not sure I want to hear the rest. It's too much. This can't be real, but I need to know the truth. My brother would have only been ten.

"They shot her. He took away my sister," Kai says, a few tears falling down his cheek.

I stand up and wrap my arms around his waist. He stays completely still for a beat before his arms melt around my back. I rest my ear against his chest, the *thump thump* of his heart the only thing keeping me from losing my shit.

Pulling back slightly, I look up into his brown gaze. I want to take it all away. No one should have to go through something like this. I understand now why he's so protective of Freya. Of women. He couldn't save his sister. She died protecting him.

"Who pulled the trigger?" I ask, and my ears begin to ring. *Please don't be my brother. I can't bear that truth.*

"Dominic did. He said he wanted to make an example of us—that it's what happens when you don't pay your dues to The Brotherhood," he says, and part of me is relieved, but the other part is angry. Why does everything have to end in violence? So many innocent lives are lost because of money.

"And your brother and his friends didn't save her, either." He steps back and keeps moving until the door slams shut. His warmth vanishes, and I'm left shivering.

It's no wonder he can't stand me or The Brotherhood. His need for revenge runs deep. They are responsible for the death of his sister, and all for what? Money. Power. If I ever get out of here, I won't allow this to go on any longer. I'm going to fight for change. For peace. And I won't stop until I have it.

CHAPTER TWENTY-FOUR

B efore
     Amirah

I sink farther into the warm water of the bath, attempting to let it drown out the heaviness of my thoughts. I haven't gotten anywhere with Jewel or the other women yet. I tried to go back to the docks today, but Gage has had the house on lockdown since the explosion two days ago. I want to be pissed at him for keeping me caged, but I get it. He's trying to keep me safe. Even if I could go to the docks, what would I do? Bill's Freight isn't there. And when I googled their headquarters, they're in New York—five hundred miles from here. I just hope Jewel isn't miles from here too. Maybe when things calm down, I can fly out and visit Manhattan just in case.

The bubbles have long gone, and my skin is pruney, but I don't have the energy to get out just yet. When my phone vibrates against the tiles of the bathroom floor, I reach over the tub and grab it.

There's a text from an unknown number. I frown, opening it.

Amirah Ledger. There's a woman tied up in a ribbon. Start looking at Magick.

I sit up straight, gripping the edge of the tub. Water splashes all over the tiles.

Who is this? I reply.

Three dots appear. My heart races as I wait for them to reply.

I helped Freya find her brother's killer, and now I want to help you find your friend.

I frown. WTF? Is this really the same person who's been sending Freya those messages? I have no idea. Should I trust them? No. But Freya followed every lead they sent her, and it helped her get answers about her brother. What if this is the information I need to help get Jewel back?

I have to try. Placing my phone back on the tiles, I step out of the bath and dry off. I know where Magick is—I've been there plenty of times but never noticed anything going on.

I should call Freya and ask her to come, but she's in no state after the explosion. She's supposed to be resting, and I don't want to burden her with this—she's been through enough. I have to go alone and find out if this leads to any information about Jewel.

Thirty minutes later, I'm dressed in a tight black sequin dress. I fasten my trench coat around my waist and grab my purse from my walk-in closet, pulling the strap over my head. My hair falls in carefully styled curls down my back.

I've racked my brain to figure out how I'm going to get out of here. I can't exactly exit through the front door. Gage would have a fit—I'm not supposed to leave. The next best bet is scaling down from my balcony. I flick the lock on my bedroom door and turn down my light so it's only a soft glow.

My high heels sink into the carpet as I make my way over to the door that leads out to my balcony. I grab the sheets from my bed that I've tied together into a rope to help me get down to the first level.

After twisting the lock, I step out into the cool night air, then shut the door behind me and lean back against the window. My heart pounds loudly inside my chest. I'm twenty-two, and I'm sneaking out so my big bad brother doesn't catch me.

I push off the window toward the railing. Placing my hand on the cool concrete, I peer over, and my stomach lurches. It's a two-story fall, and there's no way in hell I'm going to jump. I'll break a leg—or worse, one of my nails. I'm not like Freya; she loves the feeling of this thrill. I can't do this.

Yes, you can. Think of Jewel, who needs you. Who can't escape.

I tie the sheet around one of the balcony poles in a double knot, pulling tight to make sure it's fastened—the last thing I want is to fall to my death. I throw the sheet rope over the railing, and it drops with a quiet woosh. It doesn't quite reach the ground, but it's enough.

Movement catches my eye from the driveway. Headlights beam over my balcony, and I drop to the ground, peering through the railing. Gage's red Range Rover flies down the driveway and pulls to a stop outside the garage. *Fuck. Please don't look up. Don't look up and see this sheet dangling in the moonlight.* He drives inside, and the sound of the garage door closing fills the air.

I wait for a couple of seconds, but I need to move—now. If he did see me, he'll be coming up here any second. It's now or never. I push back up and hoist myself over the railing. Then I kick my heels off, and they fall to the grass below.

I grab the rope between my thighs for support, hold on for dear life, and start moving down. My hair blows in the wind, wrapping around my face. My heart thumps loudly. *Just keep going. You're nearly there.*

After what feels like minutes, I reach the end of the line. My legs dangle in the air. Before I can talk myself out of this, I let go. My feet hit the ground, the impact sending pain up my shins.

After collecting my heels and holding them. I hurry around the side of the house and pull out my wig from my bag, then stash the bag under a section of low hedging. If they see Amirah Ledger walking into the club, Gage is going to be notified right away, and that will ruin everything. I have to pretend to be someone else tonight.

Keeping to the tree line and out of the patrol's line of sight, I run barefoot toward the security gate. I grab my phone and press call on the number for the security box.

"Hello, George speaking," the guard answers.

"It's Amirah. I can see someone trying to break in from the back-yard. You need to go check it out," I say, and I'm met with silence. Shit. Will he listen?

"On it," he says, and I hang up. The gate opens, and George runs through, speaking into his walkie-talkie.

Once he's far enough away, I run straight through the gate. My e-bike is exactly where I left it in the bushes up against the fence to our property. I quickly jam my feet into my high heels, jump on, and ride down the road.

Security opens the second gate to our compound for me, and I'm off, flying down the hill toward the main street.

My chest rises and falls heavily against my coat the closer I get to Magick. The streetlights illuminate my path on one side, and cars drive past slowly on the other, music blaring from their speakers.

I've been here many times over the years. It's practically run by The Brotherhood, with members Callan and Zeke managing everything. I thought the strip club was all above board, but maybe it isn't. Is this where Jewel is? But why would Zeke or Callan kidnap her? Oh God, what if they're using her? What if she's one of the strippers, and they've got her trapped? I have so many questions—ones I intend on getting the answers to tonight.

I walk past the line that's all the way around the block. Men in suits and women dressed up in tiny dresses wait to get in. I don't want to stand in line all night. Any moment now, Gage or one of the guards will see my sheet rope and come looking for me.

I need to get in there now.

Closer to the front, there's a group of girls chatting, laughing, and taking photos together. While they're distracted, I slip under the rope and stand in front of them. None of them even notice me.

I adjust my blonde wig, one that Freya left at my place from when she used to sneak into our parties. At least it's coming in handy tonight to help conceal my identity. I wish I had my best friend with me.

Five minutes later, I'm let in, and they've got my fake ID in the system. Penelope Walter. It's amazing what you can buy when you have an unlimited amount of money, and this identity means I can be somebody else for the night.

Stepping through the curtains into the main large, open room, I blend into the crowd. The bass of the music vibrates around me. I sidle up to the bar and order an Old Fashioned. Sitting on the barstool, I watch people move around me. Talking, drinking, dancing. Nothing seems out of the ordinary.

The bartender passes me my drink and I give him a fifty.

An older guy and a young girl who looks young enough to be his daughter come up beside me. He's running his hand down her arm, and her mouth turns inward, like she's repelled by him, but then she smiles, batting her eyelashes at him.

Should I help her? Is she okay? They walk off together, through the crowd of people, past the empty stage, and through a curtain. I need to follow them. What if that's what's happening here? Maybe Magick isn't just a strip club; maybe women are being forced into prostitution?

What if Jewel is somewhere back there right now?

I push off the bar, drink forgotten, and force my way through the center of the dance floor. Reaching the curtain, I glance over my shoulder, but no one is stopping me. I disappear into a long corridor, red LED lights illuminating the path.

A door opens and slams shut. Two figures move toward me. Fuck. I keep moving, my head cast down. I need to find out what's happening here—if Jewel is back here somewhere in one of the rooms.

"You lost?" the voice belonging to the guy says, and it sounds so familiar.

I look up and almost run straight into Callan and a young woman behind him. Shit. I keep my eyes down.

"Just looking for someone," I say.

"Don't I know you from somewhere?" he asks, and all the blood drains from my face. *Run.*

Turning around, I bolt straight through the curtain, onto the dance floor, and back out the front entrance and around the corner of the building, not stopping until I'm halfway down the alley.

I lean back against the brick wall opposite the back door, hands braced on my knees as I catch my breath. That was close. Too close. Callan is one of the Brothers, one of Gage's men. If Callan recognizes me, he'll call Gage. But I don't have much time left, and I'm not leaving here until I have answers. I need to get back inside and find out what's happening behind those curtains.

I check the handle on the door. It has to lead to the club, but it doesn't budge. Locked.

Maybe someone will come out this way.

Maybe you should go back home before you get caught, Amirah.

I ignore the voice of reason. Sometimes a girl's gotta do what a girl's gotta do.

A few minutes later, the door opens, and a lady dressed in a black corset moves past me, her name badge pinned to her chest.

I reach out, grabbing her arm. She screams, but I place my hand over her mouth. Her eyes widen, and I bring my finger to my lips. She nods and I release her.

"What the hell?" she snaps.

"I need to get inside there and into the private rooms, and you're going to help me."

She looks me up and down. "And why would I do that?"

I pull out a hundred-dollar bill from my jacket pocket, and the corner of her mouth lifts.

"That'd do it." She looks up and down the alley. "Follow and do everything I tell you. Got it?"

I nod, and she takes my hand and leads me inside.

Red LEDs along the floor light the pathway. We move down the hallway I was in before, turning left, then right, and come to a stop in front of a black door.

"Go inside, and do whatever they tell you," she says, and I turn around to ask her what's happening, but she's already disappeared down the hallway.

I have no idea what waits on the other side of this door, but I'm here to get answers, and I pray to God that Jewel is there.

I open the door and step inside, shutting it softly behind me. I stare at my reflection in the mirror that fills the back wall. I count five girls sitting in booths, doing their hair and makeup, getting ready. They look strung out, broken. A lost look in their eyes. When the girl next to me places her arm down on the counter, I notice track marks lining her pale skin, and I suck in a deep breath. I don't recognize any of them. No Jewel.

One girl walks past me wearing a red silky robe. I reach out and grab her arm. She frowns, coming to a stop.

"Yeah?" she asks, her gaze roaming up and down my body.

"I'm here to work."

"Talk to Aubrey," she says, pointing at the girl sitting in front of the mirror who is curling her long blonde hair. She looks young, younger than me.

I move toward her, and she watches me closely through the mirror, her eyes moving up and down my body.

"You're Aubrey, yes?"

She narrows her gaze, frowning. "Yeah?"

"I'm here to work," I say, and Aubrey finishes curling a piece of her hair before putting the curling iron back on the counter in front of her.

"Who sent you?" she asks. "I didn't know we had any new girls starting tonight." She watches me closely, cocking her head to the side. Does she recognize me? Does she know who I am? Shit.

I lean in close, whispering in her ear. "Can we talk in private?"

She frowns, regarding me shrewdly before finally nodding, then points toward a closed door at the back of the room.

I step back and head over there. Girls watch me through their mirrors. Some are talking among themselves. They look young—too young to be working here. Have the girls been this young every other time I've been? I can't remember. What have I walked into?

After reaching the door, I twist the handle and move inside. It's pitch black. I run my hand over the wall until I find a switch and turn it on. I'm in a large closet full of clothes and toys. Lingerie of all colors, lace, and leather hangs in front of me. An array of whips and toys line the wall opposite me. Wow.

I spin around, coming face-to-face with Aubrey.

"Okay, what do you want?" she asks, crossing her arms over her chest, pushing up her bust in her tight black corset.

I pull out my phone, bringing up the photo of Jewel, and turn it around. "Do you know my friend Jewel?"

Aubrey's throat bobs. She looks from me to back outside the room. "Why?"

"I haven't seen her in months. Have you seen her working here?"

Aubrey releases her arms, rubbing her palms along her bare thighs up to the line of her panties. "Yes, she works here," she says, looking back toward the room once again. Sweat beads on her forehead. I'm running out of time.

"When?" I ask, and Aubrey moves toward the door. "Please?"

She looks back at me. "I'm sorry, I don't have much time until he comes looking for me."

She bites her bottom lip, and I fight the urge to pull her in for a hug. There's a faraway look in her eyes. She seems broken, lost, and I want to make it better. What is this place, and what are they doing to these girls?

"Who's he?" I ask, and her hand shakes.

"The enforcer is working tonight. When he's on, you don't mess around. Jewel is one of his favorites." She opens the door, and I move, gripping her arm. She flinches, and I release it. Fuck.

"Meet me in the alley to talk freely," I rush out.

Aubrey shakes her head. "I can't."

"Please. I can help," I press.

Aubrey lifts the corset a bit to reveal part of her stomach. A long, nasty scar lines her skin. "No, you don't understand—I can't." She points to the scar and my stomach drops. I'm going to be sick. They did this to her? Oh my God. This is worse than I thought.

"When will Jewel be here?" I ask, and Aubrey releases a heavy exhale.

"Come back Friday," she says, then leaves.

I came here looking for answers, and now I have even more questions. Who's the enforcer? What operation are they running here? Does Zeke know about this? Surely he doesn't. He wouldn't do this behind my brother's back. He's one of us.

It's no secret that Magick is a strip club, but it's all legitimate. The women choose to work here; they want to put on a show and get paid very well for it—or so I thought. Now, with what I've learned, nothing is what it seems. Something else is going on behind the curtains, and I'm determined to find out what.

Friday can't come quickly enough.

CHAPTER TWENTY-FIVE

Z ion

   After the confrontation on the tracks yesterday, one thing was on my mind and one thing only: seeing Cleo. But when I messaged Natalie as I jogged across the tracks and slipped into the ville, she said she'd been fired and that a new nanny was taking her place.

   I stay hidden in the bushes; there's more security around than usual. Two guys sit in chairs on the porch out front. A couple of cars are parked in the driveway. People are on the streets, looking for Amirah. I can't risk my daughter's safety by running in there now. And who knows what the new nanny will be like? Natalie told me she's from the same agency as her, but that doesn't mean I can trust her with the truth.

I need to plan this out. I back away from the house, pulling up my hood so I blend into the streets as I walk farther away from her. Each step feels like a knife to my chest.

"Hey!" someone yells from across the street.

I'm half a block from the tracks. Almost home. Fuck. I ignore them, moving quicker.

"Stop!" they say louder this time.

I keep my head straight, my hood covering my face. Then I bolt. A gunshot rings through the air. I jolt right, trying to avoid it. Goddamn it. More shots are fired. I run through the bushes, putting more distance between me and my assailant before reaching the fence. I climb and jump over. My feet land in the hard dirt as more shouts follow me.

I don't stop running until I'm back in Bear's amusement park and pushing inside his door. He's sitting on the couch, writing in his notebook.

He looks up at me. "Didn't know you were training for an iron man."

I fall back onto the couch next to him, not having the energy to reply. It takes me a second to catch my breath. Fuck, that was close. Too close.

Every second that ticks by is time wasted. Time that could be spent rescuing my daughter, bringing her back where she belongs. She was safe in Daringville with Lauren, and she was somewhat protected with Natalie. Now, with the new nanny and security, I can't take my chances. I've got this sick feeling that she's not okay with him. Everything has changed. She can't stay there with Callan. If anyone found out about her, they could use her against me—against the Hood—and I won't allow that to happen. I won't put her in the firing line.

We've already lost precious time while Kai has been with Amirah, feeding her lunch or whatever the fuck he's doing. What is taking so long? After that meeting, we don't have long before The Brotherhood will come for us. I need to get my girl out to-fucking-night. And I'm going to need all the help I can get. I inch forward on Bear's couch, my knee bobbing.

Bear kicks my foot, and I glare at him. He smirks, leaning back on the couch, and flicks his knife in and out repeatedly. "What's got your panties in a twist?"

Bear laughs as I roll my eyes. "Sometimes I wonder why we're friends."

I'm done waiting; we need a plan. Now. I jump to my feet and move through the room. Bear's footsteps follow me. I don't stop until I'm outside of Amirah's bedroom. I'm about to burst through the door when it flies open and Kai crashes into me. Bear and I stumble back into the wall behind us as Kai closes the door to Amirah's room.

"Fuck, sorry," he mumbles, wiping at his cheeks. What the fuck happened in there? I shake my head. We don't have time for this.

Bear watches him closely, his leg kicked up against the wall.

"We need to make a plan," I say, and Kai releases a heavy exhale.

"I know. Can you just give me five?" he asks, but I shake my head.

"No, we need to do this now. We've already wasted enough time," I bite out in a raised voice, and Kai nods.

"I need to speak with her," I say, pointing toward the door, and Bear kicks off the wall and comes in closer.

"Why?" he asks, all protective. Fuck me. I can't deal with him right now.

"She might have intel on Callan. She already knows about Cleo, thanks to Kai's big mouth, so I may as well use her for information."

As I reach for the door, Bear shoves me, but I don't budge.

"You hurt her and I'll hurt you. Understand?" Bear says, getting right up in my face.

I push past him, opening the door. The bed is empty. I step inside and look around. She's sitting back against the wall closest to the door, her mouth slightly ajar, cheeks pink. Was she listening to us?

Bear and Kai come inside too. Kai sits on the bed and Bear stays standing close to her. The room suddenly feels small. Tight. Amirah looks between us. She seems tired, her eyes red like she's been crying.

"What do you know about Callan?" I ask, jumping straight to the point. Time is ticking away.

"Why?" she asks, cocking her head slightly to the side.

I take a deep breath before opening my mouth. She hasn't done anything wrong. This isn't her fault. I don't want to come across as angry or forceful. I just need answers.

I step closer and kneel in front of her. She has her knees up, arms wrapped around them.

"My daughter is in his care—well, his and some random nanny's—and I need to know everything about him. Please?" I beg.

Her eyes widen. She looks at me, then to Bear next to her, and back to Kai on the bed. She hugs her legs tighter.

"If your daughter is in Callan's care, she isn't safe," Amirah says, and a mixture of emotions run through my body. She's telling me the truth. She cares. I can't deal with this. I need more. Why?

"Tell me everything you know about him," I demand, and Amirah nods.

"He . . . he isn't bad like you guys think The Brotherhood men are bad. He's different. Worse." She swallows, her gaze resting on mine. "Before I came here, I was investigating something." She watches me closely, as if she's trying to find something in my eyes.

Please, I want to beg. *I need to know what we are running into.*

"He has ties to that. With a club where they are doing unthinkable things. If your daughter is with Callan, you need to get her out before it's too late," she says and I stand up, all the blood rushing to my head. Fuck. This is worse than I thought. I should never have left Lauren or my daughter in his care.

"What kinds of things does this club do?" Bear asks, running his thumb over his bottom lip.

Amirah glances between the three of us, her forehead scrunched together. She lets out a heavy sigh. "They're trafficking women against their will."

I clench my fists, anger rolling off every fiber of my being. Fucking hell. The list of shit to do is getting longer and longer, but my priority is my daughter.

"Where is the club? How many men does he have under his thumb? What routines does he have?" I fire off, needing every piece of intel I can get.

"The club is on the main street of Daringville. It's called Magick. I don't know how many men or the routines. I was looking into this before I got kidnapped and taken against my will." Amirah glares at Bear, and he smirks, but I frown. Isn't that the club Bear helps out at for cash? Does he know anything?

"Have you been to the club?" I ask Amirah. I'll pump Bear for info later.

For the next five minutes, Amirah tells us about her visit to the club and everything she found out about what goes on there, as well as all she knows about Callan. He might be running it, but she doesn't know for sure.

"Thank you, Amirah," I say, moving toward the door.

She gets up, placing herself between me and the exit, and braces her hand on my chest. "Wait, let me come with you. I know things about Daringville you don't. And the nanny—I know a lot of the women who work in the city, thanks to the parties I've thrown that we've opened up to the general public. You need me," she says, and all I can hear is the pounding of my heart.

"Why should I trust you?" I ask, studying her eyes, searching for something within them, a glimmer of truth.

She keeps her gaze on mine, never wavering. "Because without me, you won't stand a chance," she says.

"Zion," Kai says. I look toward him, and he shakes his head in warning, but I ignore him.

Time is ticking, and I'll risk everything to save my daughter.

"Okay," I agree and push past her out into the hallway.

I'm either going to regret this, or it'll be the best decision I've ever made.

CHAPTER TWENTY-SIX

A mirah

    I lean back farther, the wall of my bedroom supporting my weight. The room feels even smaller with Bear and Kai inside.

Bear moves toward me, leaning his head against my shoulder. I want to push him away, but too many emotions are flowing through me.

"Aww, princess. I'm so proud of you. Look at you fitting into our little troubled trio." He gazes at me, batting his eyelids, and I can't help but smile. Bear may be many crazy things, but he can lighten the mood.

There's no way I would say no to helping Zion with his daughter. He needs my assistance, and when he mentioned Callan, that fueled my desire. If she's under his care, she isn't safe. I can find out more about Callan during the trip—things that could help me free more of the women in that club when I finally get out of here.

I'm not clear on his position at the club, but he is part of it, and I wouldn't want my daughter anywhere near that or him. And maybe after Cleo is safely in Zion's hands . . . I can escape too.

But if Callan is tied up in this mess with the girls, this retrieval could be dangerous. After what I found out at the club, I know they have a lot of twisted men on their team who aren't afraid to be vicious.

"Have you ever heard whispers about the enforcer?" I ask, and Bear lifts his head from my shoulder. He looks toward Kai, then back to me, before he shakes his head.

"Nah, I haven't. Why?" Kai asks.

"He's part of all this. He keeps all the girls in line, but no one knows who he is," I say, and Bear scoffs.

"Whoever they are, we'll sniff them out," Bear says, and I purse my lips.

Kai pushes off the bed and stalks over to us, reaching out his hand. I grab it, and warmth spreads through my palm. I want to comfort him after what he shared only an hour ago about his sister. If Dominic wasn't dead, I'd kill him again.

I don't blame my brother or Hazen or Lucas for what happened. They were only kids themselves.

Kai pulls me up but doesn't let go of my grip. He wraps his fingers through mine, and it feels good. Safe. Like I belong there in his hold.

Kai leads me out of the room, and my heart rate skyrockets. We're leaving? I haven't been out of these four walls for over a week, and this is what I've prayed for. Are we really going right now?

Bear follows silently behind us. I can't see him, but I can sense his presence. The more time I spend here, around them, the closer I feel to them. Do I really want to leave?

Yes. I'm their prisoner. Held against my will. But why does the thought of leaving them hurt me more than the idea of staying?

Damn, these men are confusing me.

A door slams behind me, and I jump, pulling out of Kai's grip, just waiting to be taken back to my room. Are they playing with me?

I spin around, and Bear is there, with my new favorite hoodie—the one that has the 18hood logo on it. He holds it out to me, and I take it, offering him a smile.

When I lift it over my head and pull it on, my shoulders relax.

Kai walks off ahead, and I follow closely behind with Bear next to me. We head through the rooms that I came through when I first arrived at this amusement park, what seems like a lifetime ago.

We reach the living room, and Bear shuts the door behind him. Zion is on the couch, leaning forward, resting his chin on his hand.

I stay standing, unsure where to go or what to do. Bear brushes up beside me, and Kai sits next to Zion.

"Okay, before we head over there, we need a plan. What does the house look like? Have you spoken to the new nanny?" Kai asks Zion.

I stay silent, melting into the background. Bear stays close to me, his body heat keeping me warm. I walk around the space, and there's something about it . . . it feels nice being here. Like I have so much more room to move than I did before.

Zion glances my way, followed by Kai. Oh no. Is this when they're going to send me back to my room? I can't go back. I won't.

"No. I need to reach out and find out when she's working," Zion says, tapping away on his phone.

"Who's the new nanny?" I ask.

"Rachel Saunder. Do you know her?" Zion asks, and I don't recognize the name.

"No, but we need to get the nanny out of there too. When Callan finds out Cleo is gone, he could hurt her," I say, and the corner of Zion's mouth curls.

He doesn't know what Callan is capable of. Hell, I don't either, but he's part of that club and approves of what they do to those women. He knows what the enforcer does.

"Cleo and Rachel's safety is our priority," Kai says, and pride wells up inside me. These men are messing with my poor heart.

"I could always take another captive?" Bear suggests.

"What, I'm not good enough?" I ask, and Bear wraps me under his arm. Against my better judgment, I lean into his embrace.

"Aww, you jealous, princess?" he asks, and I roll my eyes, choosing to ignore him. I won't admit this out loud, but the thought of another woman being here with them doesn't feel right.

"You said she's with a nanny service, right?" I ask.

I try to pull out of Bear's hold, but he doesn't let me, tightening his arm around me, so I stop fighting.

"Yeah, she works with an agency," Zion says, and an idea forms.

"I could pretend to be a replacement for her. Tell her to take the day off. Say she's sick," I suggest, and Zion flips his phone between his fingers.

"That could work, but what if he recognizes you?" Zion asks.

He could, but I don't want to convince the guys of that. This could be my way out. I could bring Cleo back to them and then run for it.

"Haven't you heard of makeup and wigs?" I raise an eyebrow. "I can turn from this into a different person," I say, pointing to my face.

Bear presses a sloppy kiss on my cheek, and I don't pull away or fight him. It's nice to be wanted. Back home, no one would dare just kiss The Brotherhood princess. It was always *please may I*—formal, passionless embraces that meant nothing and left me wanting.

"Whatever you look like, you'll still be my special captive," Bear says, and warmth spreads over my skin, my cheeks heating.

I'm not sure if he means it as a threat or not, but something about being anything of his feels good.

I'm in way too deep here. I need space. To get away from them. I'm not one of them. I am their property, nothing more. But why does it hurt when I think those words?

Zion's phone buzzes, and he checks it.

"Amirah, write out a list of everything you need, and we'll get it. Rachel's scheduled to work tonight. Natalie is going to get her out of it somehow. The clock is ticking," Zion says, and I nod.

Bear takes me back to my room, and I write down the makeup and the blonde wig I'll need to pull this off. I hand it over to Bear. He leaves but doesn't close the door behind him, keeping it open.

Does he trust me not to run anymore? There's no point in trying. I'd have to get to the front door still, and even then, there's always one of the boys hanging around in the living room.

I'll get my chance tonight when I'm back home in Daringville.

Chapter Twenty-Seven

B ear

She runs her hand through her blonde wig before brushing it up into a high ponytail. I don't even recognize the woman in the camera. I lean back in my computer chair. Damn, she was right. She can transform into somebody else. I don't like it. She looks different. Weird. I can't wait until this is over and she takes all that shit off.

She asked me where I got all these clothes from that I've given her, and I said I'd had them lying around. She didn't like that answer, but if I told her the truth, she wouldn't look at me the same way again. I'll never let her know my secret.

"Bear, get over here," Kai snaps, and I push back my seat with a grunt.

Zion and Kai have been busy planning out tonight while I've been glued to the computer, watching her. I left the door open on purpose as a test to see if she'd run again, given the chance, and she hasn't. She wants to help us, and that fills me with pride. My captive princess is part of our gang of misfits. I don't ever want her to leave, but whatever happens tonight with Cleo will change everything. After this, we'll have to do something. Return Amirah or somehow destroy the ville, even without weapons.

I lean back against the couch armrest, folding my arms over my chest.

If we get Cleo back, will Kai and Zion hand Amirah back? Strike a deal? Or will they send her back in a body bag? I don't believe that will happen. I won't let it. I'll fight for her. There's no way in hell I'm letting her go. She belongs with me. Us.

I won't sabotage saving Zion's little girl, but if they choose to let her go, I will fight against them. I'll ruin anything that gets in my way. Life without her in it isn't life at all. She's the only person in this fucked-up place who understands me; she really gets my kind of crazy.

"Bear, are you even listening?" Zion hits my knee.

I bite my bottom lip with a light shake of my head.

"Tate has gathered some men for us if we need them, but I want us to get in and out without too much noise. We don't have enough weapons. Remember that Cleo's safety is our priority," Zion says, gaze set on me.

"And we need to conserve ammunition for when we need it," Kai says, and I don't know if he's talking about when the boys come for Amirah or when we try to take over Daringville, but I hope it's the latter.

"Whatever, and what about Amirah?" I ask. She's all that matters to me.

"She's your responsibility. You don't let her out of your sight. And make sure Callan doesn't lay eyes on you. Understand?" Kai asks, and I nod. He's right—I can't risk being seen.

"Done," I agree. That's what I was going to do, anyway.

We spend the next hour planning everything out. Natalie has given us all the details we need. What security is where. Callan's movements. It's all set. We even plan to send Tate to get Natalie, to bring her over to our side of the tracks in case shit gets messy. Apparently, she has a cousin here she can stay with, and since she recently lost her job, it's not like she has anywhere better to be.

"Go get Amirah. We're ready," Kai says, and I skip out of the room.

I sneak into her room and lean back against the bathroom door-frame, watching her. She's applying eyeliner to her eyes, and I hate it. She doesn't need that cakey shit on her face. She's perfect au natural. I like her without it. Clean. Real. Raw.

"What do you think?" she asks, watching me in the reflection of the mirror.

I scrunch my nose. "I like you better without all that," I reply truthfully.

She frowns. "I thought guys liked makeup and blonde hair?" she asks, finishing off painting her eyes.

"Maybe, but not me. Us," I say, and Amirah smiles.

"You guys are pretty close, huh?"

"They're like brothers to me," I reply. "Not your kind of 'we're so cool and important rich dick' brothers, but the real kind. Family."

I push off the door and move in behind her. As I wrap my arms around her, she leans back into my chest, and this feels good. Right. I want to hold her every day. Like this.

"Do you have family? By blood?" Amirah asks, and I swallow hard, unsure if I want to answer her. It's a complicated question.

"I did once," I say instead, and Amirah catches my eye in the mirror. "I'm a twin, and she's just as crazy as I am," I say.

Amirah laughs. "I doubt that. Where is she?"

"Locked up. Where I should be too," I say.

"Do you really believe that?" she asks quietly.

I shrug. "Probably."

"There's a lot of wild in you." She tucks my hair behind my ear, and her calm voice—I feel it in my chest. "But there's a lot of good too."

I'm afraid she's wrong. I'm afraid I'll hurt her someday, when the voices get too loud.

I'm afraid she knows too much about me. That she'll leave at the first chance she gets.

My hand rests on her heart. The thump is heavy against my palm.

"Nervous?" I ask, desperate to change the subject.

She scoffs. "I may be The Daring Brotherhood princess, but that doesn't mean a lil action scares me." The corner of her mouth lifts into a smirk, and my cock stirs, begging to fill her. Do we have time? Would she even let me?

Don't be weak. Take what you desire.

"You're excited, then?" I ask, running my hand down her stomach.

She watches me in the mirror, shaking her head slightly. I lower my hand, inching closer to her waist. She's a liar; she wants this. I've been dreaming of touching her again. Those dreams turn into parties with my hand every night. Then I fight with myself not to come to her room and force myself on her. I've had to chain myself to my bed. Sometimes the voices get loud. Too much.

I lean down, pressing my lips along her tender neck, without tearing my gaze away from hers in the mirror. She shivers. I run my tongue from below her ear to her collarbone. Goosebumps rise on her chest, and a deep fire burns inside me.

My fingers reach the hem of her jeans, the ones that I found for her. The ones I had lying around. They fit her perfectly.

Her hand rests on mine. "Stop. We have to go, don't we?" she asks, and I breathe heavily out my nose.

"I can be quick. You need this," I say, and she glares at me.

There's a knock on the door, and Amirah pulls out of my embrace. *Grab her. We aren't finished.*

I reach out but then pull back. Fuck. I can't.

She fixes her wig, and Kai stands at the bathroom door, looking between us both with a smug expression on his face. Cockblocking asshole.

"You good?" he asks Amirah, and she nods.

"I hope this works and doesn't turn into a shootout," Amirah says.

I chuckle. That would require guns, and that's our whole damn problem. But I don't trust her enough to tell her that yet.

Kai leaves and Amirah brushes past me. I grab her arm, pulling her backward. She gasps, and my mouth closes over hers. She tries to fight me, then my fingers tangle in her hair, and she kisses me back. Her plump cherry lips are all I can taste. She pushes her chest into mine, her hand resting behind my ear. She slides her tongue against mine, and it's blessedly quiet in my head as all I hear, taste, and feel is *her*.

A deep groan rumbles in my chest, and Kai curses from somewhere behind us. I reluctantly let her go, and she takes a step back. Her cheeks are flushed bright pink.

I really hate that blonde wig on her. I want to rip it off—it's not right.

She turns and walks out of the bathroom. Kai glares at me, and I flip him off. It's no secret that she's mine. I've laid claim to her from day one, but I can see the way he looks at her. How much he's fighting with himself about her.

I don't share much, but her, I'll consider. Just with my best friends.

CHAPTER TWENTY-EIGHT

Z ion

    My stomach is a mess, and it feels like a heavy weight is resting on my chest. I peer through the trees. Amirah is on the front step, her fist knocking on the door. After receiving a message from Natalie that Rachel is safely away from here, we moved. Now everything rides on Amirah.

Callan answers the door. He looks at Amirah, then left and right. I don't move a muscle, afraid that one wrong step will ruin this, and I can't afford for anything to go wrong. My daughter is on the line, and she's my everything.

His gaze returns to Amirah, and he leers at her as he runs his fingers through his graying hair. Bear growls next to me, and I reach out an arm against his chest in an attempt to hold him back. Bear could ruin this. I get it; he's angry. I am too. The way Callan is looking at Amirah makes my blood boil, but we can't fuck this up. Does he recognize her? Will she blow this for us?

Did we trust her too easily? This is her perfect opportunity to run, to tell Callan who she is. Fuck.

Amirah tucks a strand of her blonde wig behind her ear and says something to him. He steps outside the door, and Amirah doesn't move a muscle. Fuck. I squeeze the gun tighter. I don't want to ruin this, but if he touches her the wrong way, I won't hesitate to pull the trigger.

Kai is on the other side of the house, among the trees, hidden. Is he thinking the same thing as me? That we shouldn't have trusted Amirah so easily? And she could get hurt, which we don't want either.

Callan steps back, letting Amirah inside before shutting the door. We are fucked. Do we run now? Get out before The Brotherhood shows up for Amirah? What if she turns on us as soon as she's inside and the Brothers come and hog-tie us where we sit?

"If that door doesn't open in the next twenty seconds, I'm going in," Bear whispers, and I nod because I feel the same.

The seconds tick by painfully slowly. A loud car engine comes from down the street, headlights beaming across the road. Fuck. Is that The Daring Brotherhood here to fuck everything up?

"Ticktock, ticktock," Bear sings next to me, and I keep my hand firmly on his chest.

The car drives past ever so slowly but keeps going. I release the breath I was holding.

"Time!" Bear yells, just as the front door opens.

It takes a lot to hold him back.

Callan struts down the steps, his gaze moving around the neighborhood. I melt into the shadows of the shrubbery, praying it's hiding us. He grabs his phone from his slacks and starts typing away, moving toward a sleek black car parked in the drive. He slides inside, and I don't dare move until his headlights are halfway down the street.

I release the hold on Bear, and he runs off toward the front door. It opens, and my little girl stands there with Amirah. Cleo looks up at Amirah like she's a queen, and, well, technically she is.

I power-walk across the front yard. Cleo meets my gaze, and a huge smile crosses her lips.

"Zee!" She beams, her arms outstretched.

I gather her up in the tightest hug, and she rests her little head on my chest.

"Come on. We gotta move," Kai says, pointing to the security cameras. "We don't have much time."

I release Cleo, and she stays close to my side, looking between the four of us.

"Glad you didn't rat us out," Kai says, and Amirah scoffs.

"Who's to say I haven't?" she quips, raising an eyebrow, and Bear chuckles next to me.

"I'm always up for trouble and slashing throats. So, I hope you did," Bear says, wrapping an arm over Amirah's shoulder. She tries to push him away, but he doesn't budge.

I kneel down in front of Cleo. Her stormy-blue eyes bore into mine. Her brow is scrunched a little.

"We're going on a little vacation. Did you want to come with me, and we'll pack your bag? Get all of your favorite things?" I ask.

She frowns. "Will Daddy meet us there too?"

My heart rips in two. Fuck, that hurts. But I'm the one who wanted him to play that figure in her life. To give her protection and everything she needed.

"Not this time, but I promise we'll have lots of fun together. Like we always do. Okay?" I say, and she smiles, nodding.

I take her hand, and she leads me up the stairs.

"Keep an eye out. Won't be long," I say over my shoulder, and Kai nods.

"Have you seen Mommy?" Cleo asks.

My foot catches on the last step of the stairs, and I stumble, releasing her hand. Fuck. Does she still not know the truth? This is going to be one of the hardest conversations I'll ever have to have, but I can't do it now. Not here. Not until we are home. Safe.

"Not for a little while," I say, and I want to bang my head against the wall. I have no idea what to tell her.

Cleo continues to drag me toward her bedroom. She opens the door, and her room is spotless. Clean. Nothing out of place. It feels too clean. Too sterile.

"Where are your toys?" I ask, and she releases my hand.

"Daddy doesn't let me have them out. They are hidden away. My bag is in there. The bright-pink one. I'll pick out all Mommy's favorite toys, so she can meet us there," Cleo says. She opens her closet, and I fight the urge to comfort her and tell her everything.

Five minutes later, we are descending the stairs, and I'm carrying Cleo's pink bag full of her favorite toys. She's clinging to her teddy bear—the pale-pink one that I got her when she was born. It's her favorite, she told me.

Cleo jumps off the last step and runs straight into Amirah's legs. Amirah kneels down, and everything around us disappears into darkness. Only they remain.

The way Amirah looks at Cleo like she's the world? I can't handle this. And soon, she'll be leaving—she'll have to go back to Daringville. We don't have the weapons to keep her here for good. I'm going to lose someone else I care about. I tried so hard to fight back my feelings, but seeing them together? I'm ruined.

CHAPTER TWENTY-NINE

B efore

    Amirah

I stare back at my reflection in the mirror with bright LED lights around the edges. My green eyes glisten, and I run my fingers through my fake straight-blonde wig that sits above my shoulders, watching the room go by around me. Girls come in and out the side door as if they're lost, that faraway look in their gaze. Some girls speak in another language. Spanish, I think.

It's been three days since I last came to Magick, looking for Jewel, and now I'm back again, determined to find her and bring her home to her mom. This time, I slipped right in the back door, another hundred-dollar bill greasing the way for me.

Aubrey, the girl I met the other night, sits in the chair next to mine and grabs some hair spray.

"Go to room eight. Jewel is there," Aubrey says so quietly, I almost don't hear her.

I look toward her, and she slides a key card across the counter. I grab it and shove it inside my lace bra.

"Is she okay?" I ask, and Aubrey sprays her hair without looking my way. "How old are you?" I ask the one question that's been on my mind since Tuesday, when I was here last.

"I'm fourteen," she says, and I suck in a breath. "Does your mother know you're here?"

Aubrey shrugs, studying her nails. "What mother?"

"Did she pass away?" I ask, softening my tone.

"She couldn't wait to get rid of me. She left me on the streets, chose drugs over me, and the guys at the club took me in, gave me a home," she says, and my heart breaks for her.

"I'm sorry," I say earnestly.

"Don't be. I've got it good because I'm loyal—unlike some of the others who don't want to be here. They hate it. I feel sorry for the ones who want to get out . . . and that's the only reason I'm talking to you." She places the bottle back down and turns to look at me, then grabs my wrist. "Don't get caught by the enforcer. People who disobey him are never seen again."

She turns back around, and tears spring into the backs of my eyes. She's fourteen? And this is her only way off the streets? What the fuck? This isn't right. None of this is right. I have to release them all. How many others are underage here? Do they know what they are doing? Do they have a choice? There's so much I want to ask her, so much I want to know.

"He's coming," Aubrey says, and all the girls move, rushing around the room. Aubrey grabs my wrist and squeezes. "You have to go now in case he realizes you're not one of us!" she says urgently, and I move quickly toward the door opposite the closet.

I grab the handle and turn back around. All the girls are kneeling on the carpet, eyes cast downward and hands resting on their knees. Anger builds up inside me, and I want to stay. To help. To find out what's going on. What sort of sick person would make other human beings wait for him like that? As if he's some kind of god?

Memories of Aubrey's scar flash through my mind.

The kind of person who thinks he is above everyone else.

Aubrey catches my gaze and points toward the door, urging me to leave.

Fuck, I wish there was something I could do, but I have to get to Jewel first. She's my priority. I leave through the door Aubrey pointed to and head into another dimly lit hallway. Each door I pass has a number on it. Five, six, seven. Eight—I stop outside of that one and press my ear to it.

Voices carry from inside the room. Groans too. My hands shake. I carefully open the door, and chaos erupts.

Jewel screams. She rolls off the bed, her wild red hair flying around, and covers her naked body. She doesn't look like the vibrant young girl I remember. Her body is thin. Eyes hollow. Goddamn it.

"What the fuck?" an old guy grunts, sitting up on the bed. His erect cock is on full display.

"You need to leave now," I say in a calm voice, in complete contrast to how I'm feeling inside. Angry. Confused. Worried.

"Fuck off, slut. I paid for this. *You* get lost," he says, and I take another step inside.

I pull off my wig, stepping closer as my dark hair falls down my back. "Do you know who I am?"

He frowns. It takes him a couple of seconds before his eyes widen and he rolls off the bed. He gathers up his clothes and runs from the room.

"Fuck. Sorry," he says, before slamming the door shut behind him.

Jewel stays hidden beside the bed, and I move around and kneel in front of her naked form. Bruises line her arms and ring her throat. Shit. Her eyes lock with mine, and she bursts into tears, throwing her arms around my neck.

"Amirah," she breathes.

I wrap my arms around her slim, naked back, holding her as trembles rack her body. Her tears soak my skin, and I hold her tighter. She needs me and I'm here for her.

She pulls back and watches the door closely, her brows drawing together. "You need to leave. The enforcer, he always does the rounds at midnight, and if anything's out of place . . ." She shudders and rubs the bruises on her arm. Whoever this enforcer is, he needs to die. The fear he puts in these girls kills me.

Jewel stands and grabs her clothes from the floor. She puts on her lacy nightgown, tying it around her waist.

"What's the best way for us to get out of here?" I ask.

Jewel's face pales. "I can't leave." Her bottom lip wobbles, and I squeeze my eyes shut, taking a deep breath.

I grab Jewel's shoulders gently, not wanting to scare her more than she already is. "Yes, you can. Your mom is worried sick. Come on." I step back, grab her arm, and start moving toward the door.

She pulls out of my grip and shakes her head. "I'm not allowed to leave."

"Yes, you are. You're coming home," I reply, reaching the door. My hand rests on the handle.

"This is my home. They own me," Jewel's voice is so low, I almost think that I've misheard her.

Fuck. We don't have time for this. I thought the difficult part of the rescue would be finding Jewel—not convincing her to come home. This place has brainwashed her and it kills me. How many others are just like her, not understanding what's right or wrong anymore?

I release a heavy exhale and turn back around, moving in front of Jewel to grab her hands in mine. She doesn't pull away, but her gaze is at our feet.

"Nobody owns you except you. You can be free if you want to," I say, gently resting my fingers under her chin, and I raise her gaze to mine. "Do you want to be free?"

Tears pool behind her brown eyes. She nods, and that's all I need.

I intertwine our fingers and move back toward the door. After twisting the knob, I look out into the corridor. Loud voices carry from farther around the corner, getting closer and closer. Damn it. I close the door behind me and Jewel stands there. Her eyes are full of tears. Black smudges run down her cheek.

"Is there another way out of here?" I ask and Jewel shrugs, pointing toward the adjoining bathroom. The door is wide open. I step inside, flicking on the light. There's a clawfoot-style bathtub sitting opposite the door and a small window above it.

Jewel shuts the bathroom door behind her, and I kick off my heels, then climb into the bath, reaching for the window. It's too high.

"Come here," I say to Jewel, and she joins me in the bath.

"I'm going to hoist you up. Open the window and get out. Got it?" I ask, and Jewel bites into her bottom lip, nodding.

I push her up by her ass, and she reaches the window. A loud bang comes from inside the bedroom and we both freeze, watching the bathroom door. Fuck. We have to move. Now.

"Hurry," I whisper to Jewel, and she opens the window, lifting the pane up. She pushes out the screen, and it falls to the ground outside. I boost her up higher, and she climbs through the window headfirst. Then she's out.

The door handle twists and my heart skyrockets. I jump up onto the edge of the bathtub and grip the window ledge, pulling myself up. I push my chest out the window. Jewel is standing against the brick wall, her body shaking. She reaches up for me as I push myself farther through the window, kicking my legs.

The bathroom door opens and someone curses. A hand grabs my leg, and I scream. Jewel grips my arms, pulling me out, but the person holding my legs is too strong. I'm pulled backward through the window, the pane digging into my stomach feeling like it's ripping my insides apart. *No!* I kick hard, hitting whoever has their grip on me, and Jewel pulls, bringing me farther outside.

Hands latch on to me again, but I keep kicking until I'm falling right on top of Jewel. We tumble to the ground with a heavy thud, and she groans from beneath me.

"Sorry," I say, before a deep voice yells through the window.

"Hey!"

I jump up, reaching out for Jewel. She grabs my arm, I pull her up, and we sprint down the alleyway.

We don't stop until the club is far in the distance and my lungs give out.

My conversation with Aubrey has left a weight on my shoulders. This is bigger than just one stolen girl. I'm not stopping until I save every single girl in that room who wants to be saved. I'll work to find them places to stay, and jobs they can rely on that don't mean prostitution—especially at the age of fourteen. I wanted something meaningful to do with my life, and this is so much more than that.

Those girls didn't have anyone looking out for them before—but now they do.

That enforcer better lock his doors at night because I'm coming for him, and I won't stop until he's dead and those girls are free.

CHAPTER THIRTY

A mirah

I had a plan. Run from the house, find a neighbor, use their phone to call my brother, and be reunited with my family. But that all changed the moment Callan answered the door. The moment I heard Cleo's little voice behind him, asking who was there, and Callan yelling at her to go into the living room. I had to get her out of there.

I wanted to punch him in the face. There was no way I could leave Cleo with him. I didn't trust him before, due to his involvement with the club, and then hearing the way he spoke to Cleo? It was immediately obvious she wasn't safe with him.

I stayed true to my word, and now here I am, kneeling in front of Cleo in her living room. Her dark-blue eyes are sparkling.

"I'm Amirah, what's your name?" I ask.

Cleo stares at me. "I'm Cleo."

"And who's this?" I ask, pointing to her faded pink teddy.

She looks down at it and grins. "Twinkles."

"Very cute."

"Wait until you see all my other toys," she says, and I smile.

I catch Zion's gaze behind Cleo, and the ground beneath me falls away. He looks at me with so much intensity my heart pounds. His mouth is slightly ajar, like he wants to say something but doesn't.

He moves quickly, brushing past me, and kneels down to take Cleo's arm. Then I notice the bruise. "How did you get this?" he asks, gently rubbing his thumb over the mark.

She purses her lips. "Daddy did it when I was naughty," she says, and I fall backward onto my butt. *Oh my God*. Cleo pats Zion's hand. "But don't worry, Z, I won't be naughty again."

Zion hugs his daughter, and the silence stretches out between us. I hate Callan.

"We gotta bounce," Bear says. He reaches out for me, and I take his hand, standing.

Zion picks up Cleo, and she melts into his chest, her little arms wrapping around his neck. Damn. I never got the whole single-dad attraction, but now I do. The way he protects her, like she's the only person in the world, is so heartwarming.

Kai leads us toward the back of the house. Zion follows, and I'm right behind, Bear staying close to me. We make it out onto the back patio and move past the pool fence, sticking close to the tree line. It's dark, the light from the house guiding us.

We reach the front of the house and keep moving, then head down the street and back toward the tracks. A couple of cars go past but none stop.

I should wave them down. This is my chance to flee. To run. To escape. Why am I not moving? Why can't I leave?

Cleo watches me over Zion's shoulder. She waves and I wave back. I can't leave. I could ruin this for them. I won't put her safety above my own. I can't. It doesn't feel right.

I'll have another opportunity to escape. I've gained their confidence now. I have the upper hand. This will surely give them more reason to trust me.

Why do I want them to trust me? Why do I care?

My heart tugs at the thought. When did I start to care so much about them? When did the lines become blurred? It's as though I want to be their captive. As though I don't want to leave. What the fuck is wrong with me?

I'm too much in my head, and I don't even realize that we're back inside Bear's compound. There goes my chance. Zion carries a sleeping Cleo, his arms wrapped around her little form.

Hands grab my legs and back from behind. I'm lifted up, and I scream, making Bear laugh.

"It's time to celebrate, princess!" he sings, and before I can protest, he shoves me into that goddamn slide that goes into his underground playhouse.

Darkness consumes me and I smile. He's happy. I'm relieved that Zion got his daughter back. That she's safe with him now.

Loud laughter echoes off the walls of the slide, bleeding into my ears. I reach the bottom, but I don't move. I wait until Bear bumps into my back. His legs wrap around my waist, his hard cock pushes into my lower back, and his breath is hot against my neck.

"I hate this," he whispers, and I frown. His fingers tangle in my wig, and he rips it off, throwing it away behind him into the dark tunnel.

My breathing picks up. He runs his fingers gently through my natural hair, and my eyes flutter closed. He places his hand around my stomach and heads straight for my core. He cups my pussy through my jeans, his thumb rubbing against my clit. A deep need for release pulses through me.

Leaning my head back against his shoulder, I give in, letting him have me. I'm done denying my attraction to him. Tonight, I'll let go, have fun, and tomorrow, I can return to being the captive. Planning my escape.

My stomach stirs. I'm torn at the thought of leaving here. Leaving them.

He unbuttons my jeans, then pulls down the zipper. His cold hand plunges into my underwear, his fingers slipping straight into my folds. My eyes flutter closed.

"You didn't run tonight. Which disappointed me," Bear whispers in my ear, and I smile.

"I decided that it would have been too easy. I needed a challenge."

Bear pushes a finger inside me, and I groan, leaning back into him. He brushes my hair to the other side of my shoulder, pressing kisses along my neck.

"You know I'll never let you go," he whispers, and my heart beats faster.

Why does that make me feel so wanted? Loved? Needed? I'm falling for my captor, and I have no idea how I feel about that. It's so wrong but feels so right. Whatever this is between us, it'll never last, but we have tonight and that's enough.

He picks up the speed, forcing another finger inside as he runs his thumb over my clit. Flicking. Teasing. I need more. I want more. I sit up straighter and grab Bear's hand, pulling it out from under my pants.

I toe off my shoes, then work my jeans down my legs, kicking them away. I squat and shuffle around. Bear watches me with a hint of curiosity in his gaze. He opens his mouth, and I shake my head. I don't need words right now. I need him. Inside of me.

I release his hand, and my fingers slip under his tracksuit pants, then I tug until they are around his ankles with his briefs. His large erect dick stares at me, and I lick my lips.

"Condom?" I ask, and Bear points toward his pants. I reach back, finding one in his pocket.

"You always have one around just in case?" I ask, and Bear smirks.

"Ever since you came into my life," he says, and I shake my head as I rip the wrapper off, rolling the condom over his thick erection.

I line him up with my pussy and lower myself. As his thick cock spreads me apart, it takes a couple of seconds to adjust to his size. I brace my hands on his chest. He watches me with an intensity that should scare me, but instead it feels good. Like he really sees me. Every part of me.

I lean down, claiming his wicked mouth with mine. His fingers wrap around my hair, pulling, and pain rips through my skull. I'm hurting, but I need more. He hits every inch inside me, bringing me closer and closer to the edge.

He bites my bottom lip, and blood drips down my chin. Bear's tongue slides along my lip and down.

"I knew one taste of you, and I'd be addicted." Bear grins, my red blood staining his teeth. A shudder runs down my spine.

My fingers wrap around his throat, squeezing. I bounce faster on his cock. He groans. His throat bobs against my palm. If I push any harder, I could kill him. Then I'd have my chance at escaping. An uneasy feeling fills me. I can't do that. I'm not a murderer.

Bear yanks my hair, my neck straining. I'm staring at the slide ceiling, and I'm so close. I moan. The echoes bounce off the walls.

Bear's palm lands hard against my ass, and it pushes me over the edge. I let go, my walls clenching around his cock.

I release my fingers from around his neck. Nasty red marks stay in place, and I grin. Bear forces my head down, his lips meeting mine in a heavy kiss.

"Lift," he commands, and I release his dick, squatting. He rips off the condom, then his hot cum sprays the back of my jacket.

Bracing one hand on Bear's chest, I force him to stay lying down on the slide surface. My lips wrap around his head before taking him whole, and I taste his sweet, hot cum. He groans, reaching for me, but I swat his hand away.

He chuckles. "I need you to sit on my face, princess."

I hum, my mouth full with his cock, then shuffle around on the slide without breaking contact. I release his cock before sitting on his face. He runs his nose between my folds, and I take a deep breath.

Sweat drips along my forehead; It's so hot in here, and it's only going to get hotter. I pull off my jacket and throw it out of the slide into the room, followed by my top.

Bear flicks off the clasp to my bra from behind me, and my boobs spring free, then he swipes his tongue through my pussy. Damn, he's good. I moan. I need to do something. I take him inside my mouth again, and it's not long before I'm so close to the edge once more.

A door slams shut from somewhere in front of me, and then a figure appears at the bottom of the slide.

"What the fuck?" Kai growls. He kneels, his gaze moving from my mouth around Bear's cock to my chest.

I don't dare stop, giving him the show of his life.

CHAPTER THIRTY-ONE

K^{ai}

My fingers tighten on the outside of the slide. What in the ever-loving fuck did I just walk into? She continues to suck Bear's dick like it's her favorite meal, and my cock stirs inside my pants. This is not what I thought I would be seeing when I walked through the door.

I want to rip her away from him. To drag her back into her room and lock the door. *Wait*. No . . . I don't. Tonight, everything changed. The line between her being our captive and her being one of us blurred. She didn't rat us out. She didn't run when she had the chance. What does that mean? What do I want it to mean? I have no fucking idea.

That's why I'm here—I wanted to ask *her*. To find out why she didn't run. Why she didn't flee, but now I've lost the ability to talk. To open my mouth. I'm hypnotized by her. By them together.

No one has ever had this effect on me before—made me feel like I need them, want them. She's somehow sunk her claws into my heart, and I have no idea how I'm going to remove them or if I even want to.

I've never allowed someone in like I have her. Never trusted anyone else. Until now. She's making me feel things. Do things I swore I'd never do. Spill my secrets. She's the enemy. The more I say that, though, the harder it is to believe. Whatever this is, it's more than friendship, and I just hope to fuck she doesn't make me regret giving her my heart.

Her gaze clashes with mine. There's the glee of a challenge in those eyes. She takes Bear's cock whole inside her mouth, and my breath catches in my throat. Goddamn.

Bear groans from within the tunnel, then the wet lapping of his tongue between her folds bleeds between my ears. I fight off the urge to pull out my phone and record this to watch later, but I know it'll live rent-free in my head for as long as I'm alive. There'll be no forgetting it, even if I want to—which I don't.

Amirah keeps her mossy-green eyes firmly on mine, her perfectly round cherry lips running along his cock. What I'd do to be in Bear's position, to have her taking me so deeply. I want to run my hand over my dick, but it won't be the same as having her do it.

"Fuck," Bear moans, and Amirah, without taking her gaze from mine, swallows every last drop of his release.

She sits up, wiping her mouth with the back of her hand. There's a sparkle in the corner of her eye. She braces her hands on Bear's chest and starts riding her cunt into his mouth.

Soft whimpers fall from her moist lips, and I find myself inching forward inside the slide until I feel her breath on mine. I claim her lips in a hot, demanding way, forcing myself inside her mouth. Her tongue fights for dominance with my own.

She pants, so close to letting go and coming all over Bear's face. I pull back, leaning my head against hers.

I gently place my hand on her cheek. "Let go," I command, and her eyes flutter shut.

A deep moan escapes her as her chest heaves. There's a loud slap from Bear's hand on her ass, and I roll my eyes.

She collapses forward. I catch her, pulling her out of the slide and into Bear's bedroom. She holds on to me as we move toward his bed. She falls back on it, a loud exhale falling from her mouth.

Her bare pussy stares back at me, tempting me to touch it.

"Amirah, you taste like the sweetest treat," Bear says, slinging his arm over my shoulder. I want to shrug him off, to tell him to fuck off, but the words clog in my throat. I'm too hypnotized by her. Her naked body is laid out in front of me. She's waiting for me to touch it.

"Isn't she divine? Tell me, Kai, what do you want to do to our favorite little captive?" Bear asks, and I finally shrug his arm off.

Amirah sits up on her elbows, yawning.

There's so much I want to do with her, but I can't. Not without her permission. Not without her approval. This feels so wrong but so right. Is she as confused as me? Does she feel this connection between us?

"He's just a little shy, princess. Maybe you can tell him what you want?" Bear says, sitting down on the edge of the bed next to her.

She doesn't say anything for several long seconds. Fuck. I should leave. Go. We should be planning what we'll do tomorrow—when The Brotherhood returns.

"I want a drink first," Amirah says and Bear laughs.

"Sorry, Kai, no playtime for you." Bear smirks and my fists clench at my sides.

Of course she doesn't want me. Fuck. What was I thinking?

I storm out of the room like my ass is on fire.

CHAPTER THIRTY-TWO

A mirah
Before

The shower turns off, and I shut my journal, then place it on the table next to my bed and wait for Jewel to emerge. It's late, the time stretching into the early hours of the morning. Sleep is the last thing on my mind. I want to go back to Magick and rescue all those women. I still see so clearly the fear in their eyes, the desperation when I took Jewel. They wanted to be free from fear. But I can't save them yet; I need to look after Jewel. She's my priority.

I've tried to call Lily, but her phone keeps going to voicemail. She's probably asleep. The bathroom door opens, and steam wafts through into my bedroom. Jewel wraps her long red hair in a towel. She's wearing a pair of my sweatpants and a plain pink top.

"We need to go to the hospital to get you checked out."

Jewel shakes her head. "I can't pay for that."

I scoff. "You know I'll cover everything. We need to make sure you don't have any infections," I say gently. *Not to mention, any injuries from what those men have done.*

"Some of the clients are doctors. I'm worried they'll take me again," she says, her eyes tearing up.

"You know I'll never let anything happen to you, right?"

"I just want to see my mom and to disappear," she says, and I nod.

I want to force her to get checked, but I can't. I can't imagine what she's been through, but maybe I can help. Perhaps I can find a therapist in another town—someplace far away—who'd be willing to help her, to talk to her. After what she's been through, she's going to need all the support she can get.

"How are you feeling?" I ask.

"Honestly, I don't know. I'm just waiting for the enforcer to come and take me back. I was only in there for three years, but it felt like a lifetime." She sits on the bed next to me, and I fight the urge to pull her in for a hug. I don't want to overwhelm her so soon, but damn, it's good to see her after all this time.

"What did he do to you?" I ask, though I'm not sure I want to know the answer.

"He never hurt me personally, but he scared us. Created fear among the women. He always had a knife. Taunted us. Threatened. I was too scared to disobey, out of fear he'd attack us and make good on his promises, and once I saw him shoot a man point-blank when he refused to pay his bill," she says. Her bottom lip wobbles.

"Do you know if any of the other men from The Brotherhood are involved?"

"I'm not sure—I only ever reported to Callan, but I think Zeke may have been aware," she says, and I bite my bottom lip.

I know Callan and Zeke are involved in this scheme, but if I can get the enforcer's name, too, then I can take the entire club down. I can fuck up these men who strike fear into the hearts of innocent women.

"Who is the enforcer?" I ask, and Jewel's gaze moves from me to my bedroom door and back again.

"Am I safe here?" she asks, and I place a hand on her thigh. She flinches ever so slightly, so I pull back.

"Yes, you are safe here. I promise."

Though she nods, her shoulders are tense and her hands shake. Anger boils up inside of me. She shouldn't be feeling like this. On edge. I want to take her fear away and replace it with protection and love.

"Nowhere is ever safe, Amirah. You should know that," she whispers, and I swallow hard.

"I know, but I won't let anyone hurt you again," I say, and Jewel pushes her lips together. "I don't know who the enforcer is. I've never seen his face," she says, and I frown.

"What do you mean?"

Jewel shifts on the bed, moving back against the pillows, resting her head. "He wears a mask."

I lie down next to her, staring up at the ceiling. "What kind of mask?"

"It's always different. From animals to clowns," she says, and I turn my head, watching her. Her face is as white as a ghost as she stares at the door with a blank look in her eyes.

"That's creepy," I whisper, and she doesn't reply. "How did you end up working at the club?" I know I'm pushing so much on her, and maybe I shouldn't.

"I needed money. They offered me a job at the club, stripping, but then it turned into more than that." Her throat bobs and she scratches her arm. "They forced us to sleep with the men, something I didn't want to do, but they said I didn't have a choice. If I didn't, they were going to hurt me, and I found that out the hard way. They kept us locked in a giant hall, sleeping on the floor. The only time we got food or could leave was when we worked."

She sobs, and I pull her into my arms, rubbing her back. This is crazy.

"Did you get onto my mother?" she asks, pulling back.

"Not yet, but I've got no doubt she'll be here as soon as she wakes up."

She lies back on the bed, her eyelids starting to drop. When her soft snores fill the bedroom, I let out a heavy sigh.

After grabbing one of my blankets from the foot of the bed, I drape it over her body as softly as I can, not wanting to wake her. She needs to rest.

I keep my phone close beside me as I rest my head on my pillow in case Lily gets back to me. A million thoughts race through my mind. Things I want to ask Jewel. To find out more. Who else is behind this, and what's going on behind those closed doors? I found out a little tonight, but there's more to discover before I go in there, guns blazing. I need to know the facts. But I won't push Jewel until she's ready and has been reunited with her mother.

My gaze gets heavy and everything disappears.

***

Vibration buzzes next to my head, and I groan, reaching around for my phone. I grab it and bring it closer. The light burns my eyes. Lily's name fills the screen, and I sit up straight. Jewel doesn't stir from beside me, so I silently move off the bed and answer, opening the bathroom door and shutting it behind me.

"Hello."

"Everything okay, sweetie?" Lily asks, and I rub away the sleep from my eyes.

"She's here with me."

There's silence on the other end.

"Jewel?" she asks, and tears fill my eyes.

"Yes," I say, and loud sobs come through the speaker.

"I'll be there soon," she manages to get out, then hangs up.

I rest back against the door, checking the time. It's six in the morning. We've only been asleep for a couple of hours, and I'd love to fall back into bed, but I can't. Jewel and Lily need me.

I shower quickly and get dressed in a pair of yoga pants and a crop top, then I throw on a cropped sweatshirt. I shut my closet door as softly as I can and turn around. Jewel stirs, her gaze flying open. She sits up straight, her fingers gripping the sheets. Her eyes stop on me and her shoulders deflate.

"Your mom is on her way."

Jewel wets her cracked lips. "Part of me doesn't want to see her yet. I'm not sure I'm ready. I feel so broken."

I move toward her, then sit on the edge of my bed and turn to face her. "You're not broken. It's going to take some time, but you'll find yourself again," I say, and she starts picking at her fingernails.

I want to take away all of her pain, to help her feel better, but I can't. I can be here for her, create a safe space for her to heal, and give her everything she needs, though—that, I can do.

"I'm here for you. If you want to talk or hang. Anything. Okay?" I say and Jewel keeps her gaze on her hands. "Thank you, and thanks for rescuing me. I owe you my life."

My chest burns. "There are more people just like you, aren't there?" I ask, knowing the answer but not wanting it to be true at the same time.

"Yes, but, Amirah—" She grabs my hands, clutching them like they are her lifeline. "I'm one of the lucky ones. There's so much worse behind those closed doors. The way those girls and women are getting treated. It's so much bigger than what I've gone through. You have to help them."

My stomach drops, and my hands tremble in hers. This is bigger than I ever imagined.

"I promise. I won't stop until I've saved them all," I say, and I mean every word.

She wraps her arms around my neck, and I rest my head on her shoulder. Heaviness weighs down my chest.

There's a soft knock on my bedroom door before it opens. I pull back, and Lily bursts in, running straight for Jewel. She jumps onto the bed, falling into her daughter's embrace.

I step back, giving them some space. Soft sobs come from both of them. Tears fall down my cheeks. This is everything. I feel so empowered that I can make some kind of difference in this world. Reuniting someone lost with their loved one. Saving someone's life.

This is my purpose—to help save those who can't save themselves.

CHAPTER THIRTY-THREE

A mirah

I pull the hoodie over my head and stare at myself in the mirror. I don't even recognize the girl in the reflection anymore. She's different. Changed. Bare skin without an ounce of makeup to enhance my features. I don't feel the same. I'm not the same woman who came in here.

It felt good to put on makeup, the wig, to dress up a little bit. To change my appearance. Now that I'm back to normal again, I miss my old room. My clothes. My brother. My best friend. Are they even looking for me anymore? Have they given up hope? I'm surprised they haven't found me here, in the home of their enemy—I thought this would be the first place they'd look. Do they think I've disappeared like Alec did? Do they think I'm dead? Fuck.

After tonight, everything feels a little different too. Like our world has shifted here. When I fucked Bear, I took control. He ate me out and Kai watched. The way he kissed me like I was his favorite dessert, the release—it was amazing. It felt like the first time I've really climaxed, and with my captor of all people. Then I did it again right after. What's wrong with me? I wanted Kai as well, but it all felt like too much.

I'm confused. Lost. Being with them and rescuing Cleo changed everything.

I feel like I'm part of their dynamic, like I do fit in here, and that confuses me. The journal Bear gave me lies open on the bathroom sink. I scribble down some lines, the ink bleeding through the pages at a rapid rate. I can't keep up. There's so much I want to express. To write. To let go of. To understand.

Will I like going back home? Will I belong there anymore? I don't know. I had a chance to flee tonight, and I let it go because I didn't want to jeopardize Cleo's safety. But there was more to it than that. I didn't want to leave them. I feel stupid. Naïve. I'm not one of them; I'm the enemy, remember? But why does it seem like I'm one of them? It's all too much, these feelings, these thoughts.

I drop the pen and stumble back from the mirror. My back hits the bathroom wall, tears staining my cheeks. I have no idea what's right or wrong anymore. What I truly want. It's all messed up. Everything is. I wish I never came here. That I fought harder against Bear and got away. But then I wouldn't have discovered what it's like to be part of their group.

I kick off the wall and step back into the bedroom. Zion is waiting for me, leaning back beside the open door to the room I've been staying in. The one that doesn't feel like a prison anymore.

"Is Cleo okay?" I ask, and the corner of Zion's mouth lifts into a warm smile.

"She's fine. Asleep in Bear's room," he says, and I nod.

"What about Natalie and Rachel? Are they safe?"

If they aren't, I'm walking out that door now and finding them. They both risked so much for us. Callan should be home by now, so he'll know Cleo is gone. That puts both of them at risk.

Zion watches me closely. My anxiety is peaking. I need to know.

"Natalie messaged me before. She's away from Callan, and Rachel is too. He won't be able to hurt them," he says, and my shoulders drop. It's good they're okay now—I just hope they stay that way.

"Thank you for helping me bring Cleo back," he says, and my heart rate picks up. He pushes off the wall, and I don't know what to do. I stand there, frozen to the spot.

He closes the distance between us and pulls me into his chest. My arms wrap around his back, and I melt into his embrace. The loud patter of his heart drowns out my own. Time passes by slowly, and part of me never wants this moment to end, but I know it will.

Zion runs his fingers through my hair, tugging my head back. I'm met with his dark-blue eyes. He closes the distance between us, his soft lips melting against mine gently. Slow at first. But I deepen the kiss, our tongues colliding.

The air shifts, and it feels like someone is watching us. I don't dare stop. Heat rushes up my neck, along my cheeks. I push farther into his chest. Zion releases his grip on my hair and cups my ass. When he lifts me up, I wrap my legs around his back, and we stumble into the wall with a loud thud.

I thrust against his hard cock, my pussy begging to be touched again. A clap echoes through the room, and I pull away like I've been caught doing something I shouldn't have.

"Weren't you pleased enough with my mouth on your pussy, princess?" Bear asks, a hint of bitterness in his voice.

Fuck. My cheeks burn red. I brace my hands on Zion's shoulders. He's glaring at Bear, and it's like they are silently communicating. I go to open my mouth, but no words come out.

Is this what Freya felt like when she hooked up with my brother, Lucas, and Hazen? I don't even know exactly what's going on between me and these three men, but it's something. I can't deny that.

"Fuck off," Zion finally says, and Bear laughs.

He moves away from the door, carrying a bag with him. He stands next to us and drops the bag to the ground.

"Close your eyes and open your mouth, my naughty captive," Bear says, and without second-guessing, I obey like a fucking fool. What if he stabs me? What if this is the last straw? They don't need me anymore.

I keep my mouth open, breathing through my nose.

Zion's hands stay firmly on my ass, and I keep hold of his shoulders like they are my lifeline, because they are. What's Bear going to do? The bag zips open. Something cool kisses my cheek for a second before it's gone again.

Cool liquid pours into my mouth, followed by the burning sensation of alcohol.

"Swallow," Bear commands, and I do.

The liquid burns a trail down my throat. It keeps coming, and I continue drinking, ignoring the urge to throw up. It's too strong.

"That's enough." Zion's deep voice breaks through the room, but Bear doesn't stop.

I'm going to be sick. Finally, the liquid stops and I cough.

"Keep your eyes shut," Bear says from somewhere behind me.

"Zion, drop her," Bear says, and Zion's hands on my ass release and I fall to my feet. I wobble slightly, my head spinning.

Hands wrap around my stomach, and I want to open my eyes, to see what's happening, but I'll get in even more trouble. Butterflies swim inside my stomach. They're nerves of excitement and fear.

The button of my pants opens, followed by my zipper. Fuck. Fingers hook on my pants and underwear before they are tugged down, and I'm left standing there with nothing to cover myself with.

"It's time to celebrate, and you're the prize," Bear whispers into my ear, before he forcefully rips my top off. Then he unclips my bra. I'm left naked. Bare. Vulnerable. At their mercy.

My heart pounds loudly. I should run. I should leave, but I can't move. My feet are planted on the ground. The excitement I feel isn't right. None of this is right, but I can't hide the truth.

The truth is that I think I've fallen for my captors, and I still have no idea whether I'll make it out of here alive.

CHAPTER THIRTY-FOUR

B ear

Fuck me sideways. Upways. Frontways. Upside down. She's the devil in disguise. The only person in this whole fucked-up world who has this effect on me. Who can bend me to her will. Her body is a damn masterpiece.

Movement at the door rips my attention away from her. Kai is standing there, his gaze racing up and down her body. I should feel jealous. Angry. And I fucking do, but I don't want him to go. I like him here. I like Zion here. Watching. Waiting. Playing. It's fun. We've never shared girls before, but I could easily become addicted. Watching Kai earlier, memorizing my mouth on her cunt, made eating her out ten times better.

The way she rode my cock, her pussy molding, clasping around me, was electrifying. She's a devil in disguise. I'd do anything for her. Drop everything. If she told me to kill someone, I would. If she told me to jump off a cliff, I would. She's mine, and I'm hers until the day I die. But even then, I'll haunt her.

Kai hasn't taken his eyes off her. Will he run again? He deserves his time with her too.

She's not just any random girl to share. She's Amirah fucking Ledger, and she's a queen. Our fucking queen. Forever. She's never leaving me. Us. We won't let her.

I run my tongue over Amirah's collarbone. Goosebumps rise over her chest. Her nipples harden. I look up to Zion, then back down at her chest. He doesn't waste another second before latching his mouth onto her breast.

Amirah sucks in a breath, and I run my fingers down her chest, cupping her wet, waiting pussy. I've already tasted her today, and fuck, I want to bottle up her cum to drink every day. That sweet tang. Goddamn.

Bring a bottle with you next time.

I shove a finger inside her and she moans. Kai moves from the door, shutting it behind him with a soft click. He stands next to us, grabbing Amirah's chin. She sucks in a deep breath.

"Will you kiss me?" he asks.

I scoff. He's so different from me. I take without asking. He's got to have approval. Such a fucking gentleman. What a loser.

"Yes," she whispers, then Kai takes her mouth.

I pick up the speed, forcing her higher and higher.

Her little whimpers are music to my ears. I place kisses up her neck, worshipping her like the queen she is. I need to be inside of her again. It's been too long, even though it's only been a couple of hours. I want to live inside her cunt. To feel her pussy clench around my cock. But first she needs release. Then she'll be ready.

How far can we push her until she can't take any more? That's the challenge, and one I'm going to have fun completing. I circle my thumb over her clit while finger-fucking her cunt. Her body jolts. She's nearly there.

Kai swallows her moans, and after a few more thrusts, my hand is drenched in her release. I slide my fingers out of her pussy and into my waiting mouth. Her sweet tang hits my lips, and fuck me dead. I'm never going to get over how she tastes.

I forcefully pull her away from Zion and Kai.

"What the fuck?" Kai grumbles, but I ignore him.

I pull Amirah toward the bed, then move around her, finding that her eyes are drooped. She's wearing that satisfying *just came* look. I pull my phone out of my back pocket and take a photo of her. She glares at me, like she wants to snap at me but doesn't have the energy. That photo is going to be my new screensaver.

I drop my phone onto the ground. Kai comes up next to me on my right and Zion on my left. We all stare at her, and she doesn't cower. She stands strong. My gaze moves over her naked body—her perfect tits, curvy waist, and that bare pussy. My cock strains against my briefs. We need her.

I step toward her, wrapping my hand around her throat. Her eyes widen but not from fear. My princess doesn't get scared. No. There's a challenge in her gaze. She raises one eyebrow, taunting me. Asking me if I'm going to do it or be a bitch.

How far am I going to push her today? Is she ready for what we can do to her? Or should we play nice? Be gentle?

Fuck, no. Murder her with your dick.

This girl doesn't thrive on gentle. She wants to be fucked hard. To be taken to the edge. To be begging on her knees like a junkie who wants an ice pipe.

I force her backward. She falls onto the bed, and I go with her without removing my hand from her throat. "Zion, let me take off your pants," I growl out, and Zion scoffs.

"Fuck off," he says, and I look back over my shoulder, glaring.

He shakes his head. Fucking asshole. As quickly as I can, I release my hold on Amirah and stand.

Zion pushes me away from Amirah, and I chuckle. He takes off his pants. His long, hard cock standing strong.

I watch as Amirah's gaze moves over Zion's chest and down to his dick. She licks her lips, and I can't control myself any longer. I grab my own in my hand and start tugging, watching them together, begging for Zion to make another move. I walk over to the drawer, grabbing out a condom.

"Fuck her," I grit out, handing Zion the packet, and Zion glares at me with so much anger. I shrug. He wants this. They both do, and I'm just giving them a little encouragement.

Amirah licks her lips and nods. Zion inches forward, wrapping up his cock, then rests on his elbows. He lines himself up with her cunt and pushes inside of her in one hard thrust. My hand tugs my cock faster to the rhythm of Zion's thrusts.

Amirah keeps her gaze on Zion's, and he keeps his on hers. Both seem lost in each other. A pang of jealousy runs through my veins.

I want her gaze on me. Watching me.

No. Just let your best friend have his moment.

It takes everything within me not to shove him off her and fill her with my own cock.

She bites down on her lip. I push forward, one hand on my cock and the other closing around her throat, cutting off her air supply. How long can she hold on? How far can we push her? Guess we'll find out.

Zion fucks her hard and fast. The loud slaps fill the room. Kai watches silently, as if he's hypnotized by them.

She whimpers and moans. It's music to my ears, and having Zion and Kai here is like icing on this spectacular cake. It feels good. I just want them to witness Amirah as she comes undone. Our princess. Our captive. There's an undercurrent of electricity in the room, and it's all because of her. This princess of our enemy. Who knew that kidnapping her would be the best thing that's ever happened to me? To us?

"Bear!" Kai yells, and I focus back on Amirah. Her face is turning red. Fuck. She's about to pass out.

You could keep going.

I relax my grip around her throat, and she gasps for air. Zion pulls out, removing the condom, and his release spills all over her chest. With one final tug, I follow, painting her body in our creamy cum. She's like a damn piece of art.

Her throat is red with my handprint. Fuck, maybe I pushed her too hard?

"You okay?" I ask, running my fingers gently across her throat.

She nods, and I let out a heavy breath.

"Who's next?" I ask, looking at Kai and back to Amirah.

She's up on her elbows, an angry scowl on her fuckable lips. "I'm not an object you pass around between your friends," she snaps, and I laugh.

"You don't want more?" I challenge, and there's a sparkle in her mossy-green eyes. She does, but the question is, will she admit it?

"I do, especially if it's him," she says, glancing up at Kai, whose cheeks are stained pink.

My little captive is such a good girl.

CHAPTER THIRTY-FIVE

A mirah

The way these three men are looking at me should be illegal. Kai's gaze is conflicted but earnest. He's nervous. Zion watches me with so much intensity, my legs clench, and Bear? Damn. The attention he gives me—it's like I'm the only person in the world he admires. At the start, his obsession with me scared me, but now it feels good. Like I'm special.

I'm going to savor every second with them because I don't know what tomorrow will bring, and what if this is the last night I'll be with them? I've fucked Bear and Zion, and I still want to go again. What's wrong with me? How can I still want more of them? I should be tired. Exhausted.

I edge up onto my elbows, looking at Kai. He folds his arms over his chest, his muscles bulging through his T-shirt. I reach for him, grabbing the bottom of his shirt, and he relaxes his arms. He leans over me, and I pull the material up and over his head.

His hard muscles tense. I run my fingers along each one. He flexes. Hard. Strong.

"What do you want?" he asks me, and I bite into my bottom lip.

"You." I sit up, coming to my knees. My fingers burrow into mousy-brown hair, and I force his lips onto my neck. As he kisses along my collarbone, shivers dance through my entire body.

I glance to my left. Zion's naked body is on full display. His hand is wrapped firmly around his dick. The corner of his mouth lifts in a crooked smile. My cheeks flame. I feel so seen. Every inch of me is available to them to do as they please. I should feel embarrassed, but I don't. I feel empowered. Wanted. Like I'm their everything.

Kai sucks and kisses along my neck. Bear's got his phone out, aiming it at us. I shake my head.

"Don't worry, princess. This is just for me," he says, and I have to trust him in this moment. I'm at his mercy. Their mercy.

I pull away from Kai and turn around, then lean down to rest on my elbows. My ass is on full display. I'm waiting for him to take me from behind. I look over my shoulder, watching Kai. Bear passes him a condom. Kai rips it open before sliding the wrapper over his cock, lining himself up with my pussy.

He grabs my hips and slowly pushes inside me. I groan, shifting my grip to the headboard of the bed. Kai goes slow at first, and I shove back against him, wanting him to fuck me harder. Faster. He's holding back—I can sense it. He wants to take control, but he's not. Does he need my permission?

I groan. "Fuck me like you want to."

The words fall from my lips, and before I can take my next breath, he unleashes, pounding into me with a force I can't keep up with. The bed rattles. My fingers tighten around the rails. I hold on for dear life. Kai smashes into my pussy, breaking down every wall until I'm left panting. On the brink of screaming. It's too much. I can't handle this. Him. Fuck.

Fingers grip my jaw. Zion is there. He claims my mouth with his, stealing every thought. Capturing my moans.

A warm tongue slides against my clit. Flicking. Teasing. Bringing me closer over the edge.

Kai fucks me from behind. Zion claims my mouth. Bear sucks my bean.

I can't take it anymore. I cry my release into Zion's mouth. Tears stain my cheeks. My knees buckle. Kai holds me up until he pulls out pulling off the condom, then his cum hits my back. Bear's tongue cleans up my release before he leaves me be, and I fall onto the bed.

I curl into a ball. My eyes close, lids heavy, and everything around me turns into a black void. I'm well and truly fucked.

CHAPTER THIRTY-SIX

B efore

Amirah

Seven days have passed since I reunited Jewel with Lily, and I've been in deep research mode. My brother has been extra busy since the explosion on the train tracks and everything else that is happening. All hell has broken loose. I want to get more intel from him and The Brotherhood about what's happening at Magick, but I'm waiting for things to cool down a little.

I stare at my laptop screen. My PowerPoint presentation is coming together nicely—I'm going to present it to my brother when the time is right. I've put everything that I've learned from Jewel in there about the trafficking ring, the girls who are being held against their will, and the way Callan exerts control over them. This runs deeper than I want to admit, but there are still so many blanks.

Does Zeke know what's happening in his club? Does my brother know? Is The Brotherhood a part of trafficking children and using them as sex slaves?

My breathing picks up. There's no way my brother knows about this. If he did, it wouldn't be happening. My brother isn't good, far from it. He's done some bad things in his life, but this isn't his style. He would never take women—hell, especially children—and treat them as objects.

Jewel has told me everything she knows. She thinks that Zeke has no idea and that it's all happening under his nose. I need to crack the code of who the enforcer is, but she confirmed that Callan is one of the leaders. She saw him forcing the women to do things multiple times.

I click over to the slides I've created on the enforcer. I've put pictures of various masks that Jewel mentioned, as well as info on the things she knows he's done—incite fear, slice people open. He even slit a guy's throat when he tried to get too handsy with Jewel, which she said would have been sweet if his blood hadn't spurted into her mouth. There's a big question mark in the middle of the page. Who is this enforcer? Is it someone within The Brotherhood? Is it someone from our side of the tracks or from Daringhood? Is it Callan just wearing a mask? Although why would he do that?

Jewel said that some of the girls have nowhere else to go. They are runaways from Daringhood, trying to escape a life of homelessness or parents who don't look after them. Being part of the club is safe to them—they get fed and have some purpose. That makes me sick to my stomach. Freya could have ended up there, given her mother's addiction. All these girls need somewhere safe to go. They need protection.

I slam my fists down on my laptop and push it off my lap.

"Fuck!" I yell, and my door flies open.

Three men in suits, armed to the hilt, storm into my bedroom. "Everything okay?" the middle one asks, while the one on the right rushes to stand in front of me, and the one on the left heads for the en suite.

"What the fuck?" Is this a joke? These better be strippers sent here to entertain me, but in my heart, I know they're not.

"Not a joke, ma'am. Your brother has requested round-the-clock detail for your safety," the middle one replies, still scanning the room. "Any present threats?"

"None detected." The man from the bathroom emerges, swinging his gun around like it's his first time showing his dick to a woman.

I'm so over this. There's no privacy in this goddamn house anymore. I've constantly got three security guards following my ass. I can't go anywhere or do anything without them trailing me. This will make it impossible for me to get the answers I need. I want to go back to Magick and investigate, not in disguise but as Amirah Ledger, someone people pay attention to. I want to follow Callan, see if I can find any evidence of his connection to these crimes.

I need to speak to my brother, and he'd better hear me out. I'm going crazy holed up in this prison. I storm out my door, through the corridor, and down our stairs. My security detail follows closely behind me, and the anger I feel increases with every step I take.

After opening the back door, I step out onto the back patio, the warm sun kissing my cheeks. I head straight for the training shed, where I know my brother will be. He's been practically living there this past week.

Moving through the shed, I keep my head down, not wanting to speak to anyone but my brother. I take the stairs two at a time and rip open the office door, then slam it shut behind me. My security detail stays waiting outside.

"Yes, Amirah?" Gage asks, cocking his head to the side. Lucas stands from the chair opposite Gage's desk, but I don't even greet him. I'm so frustrated.

"So, what, now I can't even go outside our front door without someone glued to my ass?" I snap, bracing my hands on the edge of his desk.

Gage leans back in his office chair. "It's for your own protection," he says, glancing at the paperwork scattered over his desk.

"I don't want to be holed up in the house all day. I wanna help," I practically whine. I've done as much research as I can in my bedroom, on the internet, and talking to Jewel. But it's not enough. I need to be around The Brotherhood to fish for more intel. Everyone talks, and someone here knows something that'll help me.

Gage moves around the desk, standing in front of me. "Absolutely not," he growls.

I squeeze my eyes shut, breathing out a heavy exhale. I need to play this smart. My frustration isn't going to work with Gage. I learned that when I first asked him if he could help me look into things with Jewel.

"Please let me do something. Anything. I'm going crazy," I say, looking up at Gage with my best attempt at puppy-dog eyes.

"Fine. Get Freya and go train with the new recruits—brush up on your skills. You both need to be able to protect yourselves if, God forbid, we can't," he says, moving back around the desk.

My inner voice screams *fuck yes*. "Thank you."

I leave with a grin on my face. I came here wanting more power, but instead I got something even better. Training with men of The Brotherhood—it's a win-win. I can learn how to defend myself, all while fishing for intel that I need to finish my presentation.

I have to save the girls at Magick. And the only way to get Gage to help me is to present evidence so compelling, even he can't say no.

Chapter Thirty-Seven

Z ion

Her chest rises and falls with each breath on Bear's black cotton sheets. My daughter is back with me. Safe. Protected. I'll never let her out of my sight again. I'm sure she's confused, wondering why she's here, but she knows me. I'm not a stranger to her. That's something, at least. Will she understand when I tell her I'm her father? When should I do that? Will she be happy here?

Fuck. There's so much that she needs to know. I never wanted to put her through all of this. If I could take her pain and confusion away, I would. No matter what I do, I'm hurting her in some way. Damaging her. She stayed with her mother in Daringville to have a shot at a better life, and look what happened. Her mother is gone forever, leaving her with a monster.

Now that she's back with me, I can repair the damage, filling her life with only good memories. Love and protection. It's all I've ever wanted for her.

Her blue eyes blink open. She looks around the room, frowning, before her gaze meets mine. Her face relaxes, and she smiles.

"Zee," she sighs out, and I can't help but smile at my little angel.

"Where's Mommy?" she asks, and my heart breaks for her.

I wrap my arm around her, and she snuggles into my chest.

"Mommy has gone, and as much as I want to bring her back for you, I can't," I say, fighting back the tears. She was my first love. What we had was everything, and I gave it all up so that our little girl could have the life Lauren dreamed of.

"Where is she? Can we go get her?" She looks up at me with her doe eyes.

I cup her little face. "I wish I could, darling girl, but she's in heaven," I say, not sure if she even knows about heaven yet.

"That's not fair," she cries, and I pull her into my chest, a tear running down my cheek. I'll do whatever I can to take this pain away from her. To protect her from ever feeling this again.

"I know, Cleo. I'd do anything to bring her back, but just know Mommy will always be looking over you, and I'm here to protect you now."

Cleo nods. "You were always my favorite friend, Zee," she says, and my heart beats harder.

She's my everything, and I'll protect her forever. It's my full-time job now, and I won't let anything come between us.

Cleo falls asleep, and we lie like that for an hour, her soft snores filling the room. When she wakes again, she sits up, rubbing her eyes. "Can we go play?" she asks, and I smile.

"Grab your dolls, and we'll go find the others," I say, and Cleo rolls off the bed, running to her little bag.

I need to get her more clothes and things from the charity store to make her feel comfortable. We're only staying at Bear's until the dust settles. Until I've got enough money to buy a bigger home for us. My trailer isn't good enough for her. I want her to have everything. Right now, it's safer to be together. I just need to keep her away from Bear's creepy rooms. They'll give her nightmares.

We head into the living room, where Bear is laid out on the couch, one hand down his pants and the other wrapped around his phone.

I pick up one of the pillows and throw it at him. He curses before noticing Cleo behind me. He sits up and waves. "Hey there, kiddo. Whatcha got there?" he asks, pointing at Cleo's dolls.

Cleo stays hidden behind my legs, peering around at Bear with a curious look in her eyes.

I don't blame her for being shy.

Bear, with his bleached-blond hair, bright-green eyes, and colorful, mismatched tattoos, does look scary. And he is. But deep down, he is a big cuddly bear to those he loves. Those who understand his crazy ass.

He and Kai are the only people I'd trust around my daughter—and Natalie. She looked after her when I couldn't. Lauren trusted her, and so do I.

Bear shuffles off the couch and onto the floor. "Wanna play?" he asks quietly, and Cleo hesitantly moves around me and sits down in front of him, passing him one of her dolls. One with bright-red hair that's all over the place.

"This is tomato," she says, and Bear laughs.

"Because of her red hair?"

Cleo nods, smiling.

The door to the outside opens and shuts. Kai walks in carrying a six-pack of beer. He passes me one, and I take it, sitting back on the couch. After offering Bear one, which he refuses, Kai places the rest in the fridge.

As Bear and Cleo start playing together, Kai sits down next to me.

"Good?" I ask, and he nods.

"Nothing's happening yet, but it won't be long. The clock is ticking. We need to figure out our next move," Kai says, then takes a sip of his beer.

I knew this was coming. The whole *what's next*. We need to make a move. All I want to do is be with my daughter, but that's naïve of me. War is knocking on our door, and we need to put an end to this. To make a claim and have more than what we've got here in the Hood. Create redemption for what they've done to us. Who they've taken from us.

"What are we going to do with Amirah?" I ask. Now that I have my daughter back, there isn't really a reason to keep her here. Apart from all of us having fallen for her.

What happened yesterday, in that bedroom, I don't even know how I feel about it. There's something between us. There's no denying that. Plus, she didn't flee when she had the chance. She stayed to protect my daughter, and that's everything to me.

"We need to hit them where it hurts. Do something big," Bear says, completely ignoring the Amirah question.

"But without weapons and ammo, we still can't do much," I say.

Kai leans forward, bracing his hands on his knees. "I've got an idea," he muses, a smile playing on his lips.

"Spill it out, sweet cheeks," Bear says. He continues playing with Cleo, and it's funny watching him with her, the way his whole body relaxes. He's enjoying this.

"What's the biggest place that The Brotherhood uses for importing?" Kai asks, and the corner of my mouth rises.

"Docks," I say, and Bear freezes, doll midway through the air.

"Take over or blow it up?" he asks.

"We bring The Brotherhood there and set up a meeting with them. Demand they let us control the docks. We haven't got enough weapons to overthrow them yet, but this will give us an upper hand. Access to the supplies we need," Kai says, and I frown.

"What makes you think they'll hand that over just because we asked? Or that they'll even meet us there in the first place?" I ask.

Kai leans back on the couch, running his fingers along his jaw. "Because we've got the perfect pawn."

The door on the other side of the room swings open, banging on the wall, and in storms Amirah with an angry scowl on her face.

"Is that all I am to you? A pawn?"

CHAPTER THIRTY-EIGHT

A ^{mirah}

I stretch out on the bed, curling my hands behind my head, yawning. Peeling my eyes open, I find an empty room. Whatever happened last night can't happen again. Can it? As much as I want it to, it shouldn't. Not before we have a chat about what exactly this is between us.

The way they made me feel—I've never felt more in control than with them. Wanted. Worshipped. My body aches. I'm not sure I'll even be able to walk straight.

I'm confused, and sex isn't going to clear anything up for me. Whatever happened between us can't last. I'm their captive. I don't belong here. This isn't my home. The more I say that, the more I can taste the lie on my lips. I don't know where I belong anymore.

I had a home inside The Daring Brotherhood, but now I don't know who I can trust. I was taught to always believe that the Brothers were good people. The best of the best. But Callan—he's a monster.

What if the only reason my brother doesn't know about the women being trafficked is because he won't open his eyes?

Here in Daringhood, it doesn't feel like there's gender inequality—then again, I guess I've only seen inside this theme park.

Kicking off the bed, I step into some sweatpants and one of Zion's T-shirts he left here in my room. I shove the bottom of the top into my pants as my legs tremble, weak.

I head out the bedroom door, shut it quietly behind me, and move through the rooms until I'm at the last door that leads into the living room. Voices carry from inside. I open the door slightly, peering through the curtains.

Bear is sitting on the ground with Cleo, playing with dolls. Kai is on the couch, Zion next to him.

"We bring The Brotherhood there and set up a meeting with them. Demand they let us control the docks. We haven't got enough weapons to overthrow them yet, but this will give us an upper hand. Access to the supplies we need," Kai says, and I suck in a breath.

"What makes you think they'll hand that over just because we asked?" Zion asks.

Kai leans back on the couch, running his fingers along his jaw. "Because we've got the perfect pawn."

I see red. I burst into the room, pulling the curtains apart with force. Cleo looks up, her eyes wide as saucers, and her shoulders drop when she sees me. I don't want to scare her, but I'm furious. Angry. Hurt. Betrayed.

"Is that all I am to you? A pawn?" I snap, and Kai pushes off the couch, stepping toward me.

I stumble back. I'd thought there was something more between us, especially after yesterday, but what a fool I was for ever thinking that there could be.

Kai shakes his head. "Of course not."

"We were going to ask you first," Zion says.

I scoff. "Yeah, right. You're just saying that 'cause I caught you. You're really going to trade me back like a piece of property?" I ask, folding my arms over my chest.

Bear chuckles. He's on the floor, playing with Cleo, and my heart melts. *No.* He betrayed me. I knew this would happen. What the hell was I thinking, letting them into my heart and pants? Stupid. I should know better.

"You really think I'd let them trade you in?" Bear asks, his green eyes wide.

I bite my bottom lip. He has a point. He wouldn't let me go. He's made that clear.

Kai moves toward me before wrapping me under his arm and guiding me to the couch. I melt into his embrace, the fire inside me dulling with every breath.

I fall back onto the couch between Kai and Zion.

"You're not just a pawn, Amirah. You're one of us now, and we protect our own," Kai says.

The corner of my mouth lifts. "What's the grand plan, then?" I ask, feeling the love between us.

"We set up a meeting with The Brotherhood. A deal. Meet them at the docks. We tell them that we'll trade you back in return for control over the docks," Kai says, and I lean into his embrace.

"I'm in," I say.

There's no way my brother will give up the docks for me. I'm one person, and the docks are huge—a massive source of income from weapons and drugs for The Brotherhood.

And something else too.

Women are trafficked there.

I don't know how, but surely if I have all these important men there together—Gage, Hazen, and Lucas alongside Kai, Zion, and Bear—I can convince them that we can stop this child abuse. And maybe then, in our common hatred . . . we can find peace.

I'll be the pawn in this war between our worlds.

CHAPTER THIRTY-NINE

Kai

The meetup is set for five o'clock. I've got all our men assembled as close to the docks as possible, knowing that The Brotherhood has done the same. If anything goes wrong, they have my approval to start blowing it all up. I hope it doesn't come to that. They *have* to hand over the running of the docks to us. We have the perfect pawn, after all.

Every time I think about Amirah going back to them, it breaks a part of me that I don't quite understand. This was the plan all along—to keep her as a pawn. To hold her captive and use her when the time was right, but now everything has changed. My stupid heart fell hook, line, and sinker for her. Life without her here won't be the same, but setting her free doesn't mean she won't come back to us, does it?

That's the question that's been rolling around in my head. Will she ever come back to us? Does she want to? I'd like to think that she does. That this won't be the end of everything between us. She's always got a bed here if she needs it. That's one promise I'll give her.

I hate the thought of using her like this, trading her back to them like she's a piece of property. But we don't have a choice. I hope she understands. She agreed to it, so she must. It feels like she's one of us now. I want to protect her, like I do my best friends.

I couldn't save my sister or Freya. Now I'm handing Amirah back over. Maybe she's better off back home with her family. But why does that crush me in a way I've never felt before? It's as though every girl in my life has left. Now I'm the one handing her over.

I step outside, lifting my hood to cover my head. Bear, Zion, and Amirah are huddled around my car. Amirah is leaning back into Bear's embrace. She's got on her 18hood hoodie, and I want to take a photo of this. Of her with my best friends. She looks like one of us. Like she belongs here, and she does.

If you'd asked me all those weeks ago, I would have laughed at the idea. Who knew the princess of The Daring Brotherhood would fit with us? A bunch of misfits just trying to survive in this fucked-up town on the wrong side of the tracks.

Amirah looks over at me, the corner of her mouth lifting, and I can't help but smile back. She pushes off the car and stalks toward me. Before I can take my next breath, she wraps her arms around me, and I freeze for a second before hugging her back.

She rests her head on my chest, her ear on my heart. I hope that this isn't goodbye forever. That this won't be the last time I touch her.

I press a kiss on her head, and she looks up. Her green eyes are glassy. Something passes between us—a farewell of sorts.

I've spent my whole existence hating her family, The Brotherhood, for what they did to my family. To my town. And now I've fallen for their princess.

She reaches up, planting her plump lips on mine, and I savor her sweet taste, groaning into her mouth. She pulls back, breathless. "Thanks for not killing me, I guess."

I laugh. "Thanks for being a good captive, I guess," I say, shrugging.

"Hurry the fuck up. We've got a deal to broker," Bear yells. I look over, and he's bouncing from one foot to the other.

If The Brotherhood really does accept our deal, and Amirah goes back with them, I'm worried about how Bear will react. He's obsessed with her. Will he cause chaos and ruin everything? We have to take that risk. Having control over the docks will change everything for us. Give us some power back. A foothold. He'll just have to trust that Amirah will return to us.

We all will.

We walk back over to the car and pile in. I wrap my fingers around the steering wheel, watching Amirah in the rearview mirror as I reverse out of the parking lot.

She's looking out the window, taking everything in. There's a little crease between her eyebrows. Zion rests his hand on her knee. We've left Cleo with her babysitter, Natalie. She's the only person outside of us that Zion trusts with her, and Cleo knows Natalie.

I worry about his little girl. The changes. Finding out her mother is gone forever. It's not going to be an easy road for her here with us, but it's better than being with Callan.

The car remains silent the whole trip over the tracks and into the docks. Two large ships sit idle in the bay. Containers are being lifted off and placed down on the port. All of this could be ours today if this plays in our favor.

We pull up next to a deep-red Bugatti La Voiture Noire, and I want to open my door into it, scratch it up, but it won't matter to them. They'll just pay to get it fixed. The amount of money they have is ridiculous compared to the people in Daringhood, and they don't give a shit.

"Do you think there are women in those containers right now?" Amirah asks, pointing to one with Bill's Freight on the side.

I shrug. "Who knows?" But then I wrap an arm around her. "If there are, we're about to save them. We're going to take over—they'll want you back."

She goes to open her door.

"Wait," I say, and she pauses.

"Whatever happens, you'll always have a safe place with us," I reassure Amirah, watching her in the rearview mirror.

A tear falls down her cheek, and she wipes it away. "I know," she says quietly.

Bear groans before sliding out the passenger side and slamming the door. The car shakes, and I curse.

"He going to give us trouble?" Zion asks.

"When doesn't he?" I quip, and we follow him out.

The sun starts to set on the horizon, the orange glow reflecting off the water. It's eerily quiet. Amirah stays close beside me. Looking around the dock, I try to spot any of our backup, but I can't see them, which is good. If I can't, that means The Brotherhood can't either.

A scream bellows from across the port, and Freya comes running out from behind one of the containers, headed straight for us. Her long brown hair is flying behind her.

I smile. Fuck, I've missed my best friend.

She runs straight into Amirah, lifting her up and spinning her around. Amirah laughs. I leave them to their little reunion, keeping close to Amirah, not wanting Freya to take her and ruin everything. Freya lets her go, and then she turns toward me.

Her fist swings straight at my stomach. Oh, fuck.

CHAPTER FORTY

Amirah

Freya hits Kai straight in the gut. He stumbles backward, groaning, and I smile. That's my best friend.

"What the hell were you thinking?" she snaps at him, folding her arms over her chest.

"You know this wasn't my idea," he says, and Freya glares at Bear, clearly putting two and two together.

He simply shrugs, then winks at me. My cheeks heat.

Freya looks between us, frowning, and shakes her head. "You could have not taken her, too, but you did."

Lucas, Hazen, and my brother come up behind Freya. Gage looks furious. He pushes past the guys and heads straight over to me, scooping me into his arms. I hug him back. I've missed him and his grumpy butt. He releases me all too quickly. There's a softness in his green eyes that I hardly see anymore.

"You good?" he asks, checking over my body, and I nod.

The softness disappears before morphing into anger. He moves back in line with Lucas and Hazen, tugging me along with him. But Bear wraps his arms around my stomach, pulling me back, and Gage curses, releasing me. I fall back next to Bear and Kai.

"I'm going to kill you all for taking her. For lying and deceiving us," Gage snaps.

Lucas grabs Freya by her waist, bringing her back to his side.

"But you won't," Kai says.

Gage scoffs. "You've got one minute to plead your deal before all the gloves come off."

"Or we could play first?" Bear says, bouncing from one foot to the other.

Bear drapes an arm over my shoulder, and Gage watches him closely. His fingers move ever so slightly toward his gun. I shake my head at him. I don't want this to end in violence.

My heart beats faster. I'm stuck between wanting to run toward my family and staying here with the three men I've fallen for. I can't believe we've come to this.

Bear grabs my hand, interlacing his fingers with mine. Freya's gaze is locked on our hands together, and I don't move. I hold on tighter, like he's my lifeline.

Freya cocks her head to the side, and I press my lips together.

"Let us have control over the docks, and we'll give you Amirah back. Unharmed," Kai says.

"That's taking away a shit ton of our cash and livelihood." Hazen points out the obvious.

I release Bear's hand, take one step forward, and point my finger at my brother's chest. "Do you know about the girls?"

Gage scrunches up his face. "What the fuck are you talking about?"

"There were a bunch of girls in Bill's Freight containers. Being trafficked against their will," I snap.

"Amirah, enough with your silly little theories. That's not what's happening. Not under my nose."

I cross my arms over my chest, letting out a loud exhale. Fucking asshole. Is he so naïve to the fact that shit goes on under his command? That not everyone is bowing down to The Brotherhood?

"You don't—" I start, but Gage talks over me.

"We'll talk about this later!"

With a huff, I practically stomp back next to Bear and Kai. I'm furious. I want answers about those women—now.

"Ticktock. Clock is about to buzz," Bear sings, and I want to slap him. This isn't the time to be a smartass.

My hands are shaking at my sides. There's no way that my brother is going to give up the docks for me. It'd be foolish. Stupid.

"We'll have to discuss the conditions, but you've got yourself a deal," Gage says, and time seems to slow down.

He's doing it.

He's giving up their income . . . their control . . . for me.

Women don't have control in The Brotherhood. But maybe I can have some. Maybe this is the best chance I'll have to be listened to by the people who make the decisions.

"Gage, if you really want to do this, you need to listen to me," I plead with him, needing him to hear me. "There are girls being trafficked here, right under your nose. You have an opportunity to save them."

Gage snorts. "If they even exist."

"Babe, listen to her," Freya says quietly, and my brother flicks his glance between the woman he loves and me.

"You have a chance to save these girls now. Right now!" I yell, and on the inside, I'm begging, begging for my brother to hear me, for him to prove to me that my voice—any woman's voice—won't always be ignored by people in power, simply because I have a vagina.

Time stretches out endlessly, and for a second, I think he's going to do it. He's going to listen. He'll tell me he'll check the containers right here and now.

Then he frowns. "We'll discuss this later," he snaps, waving me over.

I shake my head, my nails digging into my palms. "How could you?" I ask, my voice breaking.

"We don't know for certain what's happening with Bill's Freight. It's only your word; we don't have any concrete evidence. Now, get your ass over here," Gage says, and I'm done.

Fuck them. Fuck this.

"I'm not coming home!" I yell, and I do the only thing I can think of. I run in the opposite direction. Away from my family, away from my captors.

I'm free.

CHAPTER FORTY-ONE

B efore
  Amirah

The pen in my hand flies over the page, pouring out everything that I'm feeling. The anger. The helplessness. The passion to save these girls. The heartache. The drive. Gage is making it impossible for me to get out of here and go back to the club to get more information.

I've been to one training session and tried asking some of The Brotherhood soldiers about the club, but they didn't give me anything. I'm going to keep trying. My presentation is almost ready to show my brother. Once he knows, he'll be able to help me—but will he ever really listen? Will a woman's voice ever be heard at a man's table?

I'm starting to wonder. Does he keep me around, keep me safe, because I'm his blood—but doesn't really value me as a person?

My phone vibrates next to me, and I pick it up and open the message.

Gage: Freya's been kidnapped. Be on alert. Don't do anything stupid or reckless. Stay put.

I drop the pen in my hand and stand, my journal falling to the ground. Shit. My heart races as I pace across my room and back, gripping my phone. Freya's in trouble. Gage told me to stay put, but I can't. I need to help.

I grab a black hoodie from my closet and throw it and sneakers on before heading out my door. Two of my guards push off the opposite wall. I don't bother telling them anything. I race down the stairs, taking them two at a time. Voices carry from the ground level. There are soldiers everywhere, grabbing weapons from the living room.

Ronald, one of Gage's elite, barks orders. He looks up, our eyes clashing, and stalks toward me.

"Where are you going?" he snaps.

"Tell me where they are," I growl.

"I don't take orders from you."

I grab his forearm, digging my nails in. "Gage asked me to come but didn't have time to tell me where. So you either tell me now or deal with him later," I say, holding his gaze. It's not true at all, but I don't care.

He yanks his arm out of my grip. "The home Freya grew up in Daringville."

I'm out the front door, running toward the garage, clicking my fob. The gate takes several long seconds to open. *Hurry up*. My hands shake. The front door to the house slams shut, and I move like lightning is up my ass, ducking under the garage door. Running toward my car, I unlock her as I get close, then slide inside.

Kicking her into reverse, I back out, skidding to a stop outside the garage. My guards chase after my car, but I lose them in the dust, flooring it down the driveway and out the second gate. I press my fob to open the next gate to our community. It opens and I drive out.

A figure emerges from the guard box, my lights illuminating Lucas. I slam on my brakes and curse. He looks bad. Blood stains his shit, and his face is covered in dirt.

My passenger door opens.

"What the fuck happened to you?" I ask, eyeing him up and down.

"Long story. Where are they?"

"Get in," I snap, and Lucas jumps in my car. I take off toward Freya's old house.

"Dominic has Freya. The guys are there, and shit's fucked up," I explain.

I hope we make it in time, but what are we walking into? Are they okay? My fingers tighten around the steering wheel. I can't live without my brother, Freya, and hell, even Hazen. They are family.

I slam on the brakes outside of Freya's old family home and jump out.

"Go back home, Amirah. I've got it from here," Lucas says. "The first lady of The Brotherhood can't be out on the streets unprotected. Shit's about to explode, and you can't be in the middle of it."

I shake my head. "No."

Lucas moves around the car to stand in front of me, blocking me from going any farther. He pushes me back into the front seat of my car. "Go the fuck home. Now!" he growls.

I huff, slamming the door shut. Lucas walks off as more cars arrive around me. Backup is here. Fuck, I want to do something to help, but there's no way they'll let me inside the house.

When Lucas disappears inside the home, I drive off with anger coursing through my entire body. My phone vibrates, and I grab it from the console.

Unknown - Want to help those girls?

I keep my eyes on the road as I quickly type back.

Me - Yes. Who is this?

Unknown - All you need to know, Amirah Ledger, is that they are recruiting more kids. Get to Magick at 6 am and bring backup. Answers await you.

Me - Thank you

Unknown - Oh, and Amirah, don't let the enforcer catch you, or you'll end up buried with the others.

Goosebumps scatter along my skin.

I arrive back at the gate, and security lets me in. Though this is the breakthrough I've been waiting for, it couldn't have come at a worse time. I pray that my family makes it out alive, and then we can save them.

I park back inside the garage and hop out of the car. As I move inside the house, it's quiet. Everyone is gone. I run up the stairs. When I reach the top step, a door shuts from the ground floor, and I stop. I thought everyone had left? Might just be one of the workers or my guards. They might have stayed.

Shaking it off, I reach my bedroom door. A shiver runs down my spine. There's someone here. I turn around, but the hallway is quiet.

Fuck, I'm losing it.

I open the door and gasp, almost jumping out of my skin. One of my maids is inside my room, making my bed.

"I'm so sorry," she says, her hands trembling at her sides. She's been working for us for months, and I don't even know her name. I'm such a terrible person.

"It's okay. What's your name?" I ask and move into my closet, grabbing some cash from my sock drawer.

As I return to my bedroom, she finishes making my bed. She's young, in her early twenties. She shouldn't be here working for us; she needs to get out of here and travel. Escape.

"It's Beth."

"Here, take this," I say with a smile, handing her a stack of cash. It's not much, but it's something.

Her eyes widen, and she shakes her head. "I couldn't. That's too much."

I push the cash into her chest. "Take it, or I'll fire you," I say, more serious this time.

She nods, taking the money and putting it into her apron pocket. Her arms fly around my waist, and I stumble backward a step. "You have no idea how much this is going to help me and my family," she says, and my heart breaks.

It's the least I can do. I pray that she'll use this money to have a better life and not get caught like those other girls.

She leaves, and I fall back onto my bed, releasing a heavy sigh.

Everything is about to change, and I won't stop until I've saved every last one of those girls.

Grabbing my phone from my pocket, I check the time. It's just past midnight. My stomach is a mess of worry for Freya, my brother, Hazen, and Lucas. Will they be okay? I'm furious at Lucas for sending me home. And now with the clue from that unknown number, I have to save them. I need to go to Magick.

I open a text to my brother.

Me - Update? I'm going to Mag—

The door kicks open, and my gaze clashes with a large figure before I scream, my phone dropping to the floor.

"Who the hell are you?!"

Chapter Forty-Two

B ear
        Amirah runs away, heading straight for the containers lining
the shoreline.

"Deal's off," Gage says, and Kai steps forward, anger radiating from
him.

I pull out my knife, flicking the blade between my fingers, ready
for war. One move, and I'm spilling blood from veins. Preferably his.
How dare he treat my girl like that? Like she's his property? I mean,
she's mine. Not his.

"Not our fault the princess of The Brotherhood doesn't want to
come home," Kai says, and Gage reaches for his gun, fingers hovering
over his waistband.

Ticktock, ticktock. One more move and we strike. Wait. No. Yes.

I fight with the voices inside my head, bouncing from one foot to the other. Freya catches my gaze, and she shakes her head ever so slightly. As if she can keep me from reacting. Silly girl.

"You turned her against us. All gloves are off." Gage pulls out his gun, then all hell breaks loose.

Men from The Brotherhood, I think, come out from all directions, heading toward us. Let the fun begin.

I grin, spinning around in a circle. "You're all dead!" I yell, and strike toward Lucas, my pretty little pup.

He dives out of the way, landing a punch to my side. I don't move a muscle. What a weak pup. I thought he was stronger than this.

"Find Amirah! Get her to safety!" Zion yells at me from somewhere behind me. He's fighting with Hazen.

I focus back in on Lucas. I can't let him go yet. Not until I get my revenge on him. He ran away from me. We weren't done playing. We aren't done. Not until I have the last say.

We work our way closer to the water's edge, right near one of the docked boats. Lucas lifts a gun from his waistband, aiming it at me. Will he shoot? Won't he? Guess I'll find out how he's going to play.

The ground shakes, and I lose my balance, falling to the hard concrete. Pain grazes my cheek and legs. There's a loud splash. I struggle to stand, glancing around. Containers are on fire, and half the dock is destroyed. Fuck, yeah. I grin. Now, where's Lucas?

I look over the edge and into the water. There he is, struggling to swim. Zion's voice comes back into my head. *Find Amirah, get her to safety.*

I look around. Men are fighting everywhere. Daringville against Daringhood. I wanna shed blood, but I need to find Amirah. She's my priority. I won't let her go. I can't. I catch a wave of long brown hair running into one of the burning containers. Goddamn it. Why is she playing the hero? Does she think there are prisoners in there? Naughty princess.

I run through a sea of people, sliding my knife through anyone who gets in my way. Blood splatters all over my arms and T-shirt, painting me red. The metallic smell touches my lips. I lick, and a shudder rolls through me. Fucking perfect. The best cocktail. Fresh blood. I'm an animal looking for its prey, and anyone in my path is dead.

I reach the container I saw Amirah disappear into, and she comes running out with a bunch of women and children, screaming. Fuck. I need to get Amirah away from all this. From danger.

I grab Amirah by her arm, and she glares at me, trying to pry herself away. "We need to get them out," she says, and I shake my head.

"No, you need to get out of here. It's too dangerous. I won't let you get hurt," I say, but she yanks out of my grip.

"Get them all out, then we go," she snaps, and I can't argue with her. Not when she's got that look of determination in her eyes. I'd have to knock her out and steal her for that to happen.

That's not a bad idea.

No, I can't do that. She wins.

I stumble inside, getting everyone I see out of the container and toward the water. There are a couple of girls helping, and I recognize one of them. She sees me and frowns. Does she recognize me too? She keeps moving, and I let out a heavy breath. She doesn't.

Amirah gets the last of them out and walks toward me as another deafening bang rumbles beneath my feet.

Amirah goes down, and I catch her, pulling her away from the container. People are running around everywhere. I lead us toward Kai's car, but there's nothing left of it. Half of the vehicle is on fire. Fuck.

Smoke clings to my lungs. Amirah coughs, trying to cover her nose. I leave her and run into the smoke, prying open Kai's trunk with my hands. The front half of the car is on fire, the flames getting closer. I reach inside for something to cover Amirah's nose and mouth with.

My fingers grab whatever I can and pull it out. Bottles. Bags. I reach into one of the bags, and bingo. Balaclavas. Two of them. I throw the bag away and run back out of the smoke. A second later, there's a loud boom, and Kai's car flips over, completely destroyed.

Amirah is where I left her. I pass her a mask, and she puts it on. I fasten mine, closing out the smoke. We run.

I catch sight of Zion fighting with Hazen. A loud bang bleeds through my ears, and Zion goes down. Holy shit. No.

Amirah screams, trying to run to him, but I can't let her go. We need to leave. Safety. Now. I'll come back for my best friend. His body lies still on the ground. Fuck. This isn't good. I love him. But I remember what he said to me. *Get Amirah out.*

I run, pulling Amirah along beside me, through our men and The Brotherhood's. I shove my knife inside anyone who gets in our path. Pain pierces through my skin. Something hits me, but I can't stop. Not yet. I keep moving.

We reach a forest clearing. One of the girls who helped Amirah before runs out in front of us, leading us toward a tree line.

What's beyond that, I don't know, but it's safer than here. We reach the trees and keep running until we're deep in the forest, the sounds of fighting getting quieter the farther we get from the docks.

Amirah stops running, and I brace my hands on my knees, catching my breath.

The girl with Amirah turns around and screams, pointing straight at me. What the fuck is her problem?

Amirah follows her gaze, looking between me and her. "What?" she asks breathlessly.

"It's him!" she yells, and suddenly, I know why she looks familiar. *I need to kill her.*

CHAPTER FORTY-THREE

A mirah

Bear takes a step toward Jewel, gripping the knife in his hand. What the fuck is he doing?! And what is Jewel saying—it's him? Who?

Is Zion okay? I need to get back to them. To make this right. This happened because of me. It's all my fault. Goddamn it.

I step out in front of Bear, bracing my hand on his heart to stop him from advancing.

"Don't listen to her," Bear says, his eyes turning dark. He pushes into my hand, but I hold firm, needing to hear what Jewel is going to say.

"Who?!" I ask, staring at Bear and flicking a glance back to Jewel, my oldest friend, the girl I saved.

"He's the enforcer!" she yells, and the ground beneath me swallows me into the depths of hell.

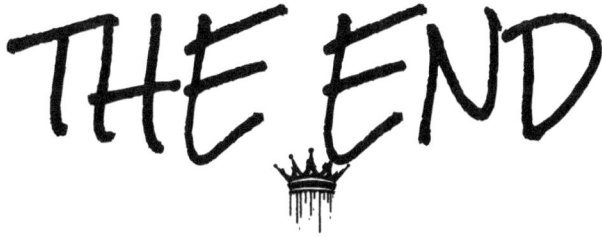

T o be continued in Deadly Little Escape pre-order https://bo
  oks2read.com/deadlylittleescape

Want more from Jenna Daring?

Join her Patreon The Dare Vault for access to exclusive stories,
behind the scenes, limited editions, story updates, bonus scenes! This
is her inner circle. Join here https://www.patreon.com/c/jennadarin
gauthor

Connect with Jenna Daring

www.instagram.com/jennadaring

https://www.tiktok.com/@jennadaring

Freebies & Special Editions

www.thedaringbookshop.com